*Side Piece Chronicles*

2

Joi Miner

*Side Piece Chronicles 2*
*Book 2 of Side Piece Chronicles Series*
Copyright © 2016 Joi Miner
Published By: Southern Goddess Ink
All rights reserved.

# Synopsis

In this episode of Side Piece Chronicles, Tyrone Price finds himself torn between Samantha, the mother of his unborn twins, and Tammy, the woman his heart desires. However, Samantha's husband, Anthony refuses to let his wife go so easily..

*This entire series is dedicated to*
*Ashley Foster aka Ghetto Angel*
*I love you! You're gone but never forgotten!*
*Another angel got her wings.*

March 19, 1987 – September 13, 2015

# Contents

# Prologue

*Samantha*

Court adjourned and everyone filed out of the courtroom. I had a front row seat to the variety of faces walking out. Some were smiling because they, or their loved ones, had been allowed to keep their freedom. Others were wearing sullen faces. Probably because they'd been fined, or their loved ones had been escorted to the back for an allotted amount of time. My eyes darted through the flood of faces, searching for familiar ones. Beth, the server from the Egg & I, who had come to court with Delilah, walked out. Beside her was the attorney that had motioned for Delilah to come to the side room in Tyrone's case. They were speaking in hushed tones and Beth's nose was red like she had been crying. Sheila, Anthony, Tyrone, and Tammy came out not too far behind them. Their faces showed mixed expressions. Tyrone made a beeline to me, wrapping his arms around my waist.

"Let's go home," he leaned down and whispered in my ear.

"Ok," I agreed, leaning in and breathing him in.

We all walked out into the midday sun. Tammy and Sheila stood just away from the stairs, chatting. Anthony stood, awkwardly, near them. Tyrone and I walked over to say their goodbyes.

"I'm going to take a hot shower and sleep in *my* bed," Tyrone interrupted, smiling.

"Good!" Sheila smiled back at her brother and looking at me with grateful eyes, "I'll call ya later."

Tyrone kissed his sister on the forehead then turned and gave Tammy a tight hug and a kiss on the cheek.

"It was great meeting you, Sam," Tammy said, smiling and extending her right hand.

"You, too," I shook her hand, smiling. "We should get together soon," I offered, looking at Sheila, "all of us."

"Sure! Let's have a girl's night next week," Sheila beamed.

Anthony stood in the background, looking like he was going to be sick. He and Tyrone exchanged a nod. I could tell he was getting angry as he watched *his* wife and

Tyrone walk to my car. I gave Tyrone the keys to the red Mustang that was identical to my husband's and stood by the passenger door, waiting for him to unlock it for me. I looked back at my husband before getting into the car. The look seemed to give him hope. I was definitely confused.

## *Sheila*

I saw Anthony watching Sam and Tyrone walk and drive away. I kept talking to Tammy, hoping my friend didn't notice. The sad expression on Tammy's face showed that she had caught it, too. Something inside of me ripped open and started bleeding. I knew Anthony wasn't done with Sam. I wondered how much embarrassment, how many lonely nights, how much back and forth I would be able to take before I finally either broke completely or just left Anthony alone for good. All I could think about was the fact that I may have cancer and didn't want to go through it alone. Until I broke, Anthony would have to do.

"I'm headed to the house, baby girl," Tammy interrupted my thoughts. She leaned in to kiss me on the cheek, "I've gotta work tonight."

"Ok," I returned the kiss, "I've got to rest, too. I haven't slept well with Ty being locked up. Felt like it was kinda my fault, ya know?"

"Nobody blames you, Nel," Tammy said, looking at me, concerned, "for either time." She looked me in the eyes to make sure the meaning sank in.

"Love you, Tammy," I said, hugging her again.

"Love you, too, baby girl," Tammy said, turning to leave. She turned back around and looked at Anthony.

"You be good to her, ya hear," Tammy said, more as an order than a request.

"I will," Anthony said, stepping up and wrapping his arm, protectively, around my waist.

Neither of us believed him.

# Side Piece Chronicles
# 2

*Tammy and Tyrone*

# Tammy

I walked into our apartment and Tre sat up from his spot on the sofa. He always slept there when I wasn't home.

"Hey, baby," I said, smiling at the fact that he can't sleep in our bed without me. Or anybody else's bed, for that matter. All the times he cheated on me, he'd always come home to sleep. As small as that may be to some, it meant a lot to me. I found my rainbows where I could in this fucked up situation I was in.

"Your boyfriend get his freedom papers or you gone be sneakin' off to visit him again?" Tre asked sarcastically.

"I don't have another boyfriend, Tre, side hoes are your thang," I said, frustrated, "but Tyrone was let go and Delilah's ass got ninety days, three years' probation with community service, and a ten thousand dollar fine."

"Damn," Tre said, standing up, "what the fuck did she do?"

"See, you don't listen to me. As soon as I mentioned Tyrone, you turned your fuckin' ears off. She beat the hell out of Nel that night we went and got Jeff. They hit her with Felony Assault in the Second Degree. If her girlfriend's dad hadn't been a lawyer, her ass probably wouldn't have gotten off as easily as she did."

"Or if her Juvie record wasn't sealed," Tre pointed out, walking down the hallway to the bedroom.

I followed him, knowing he was ready to get some real sleep.

"I'd forgotten all about that," I said, shaking my head.

"That bitch is a waste of a good body," Tre said shaking his head. "I'm so happy I picked you."

I laughed. "You only picked me 'cause she held your dick at gunpoint when she caught you fuckin' her momma."

"That shit ain't funny," Tre said, turning to stare at me, "that hoe is certifiable. She burned that damn house down with her momma in it!"

"I remember, Tre," I said, frowning, "I was the one visiting her in Psych Ward. She had a hard life."

I started to undress so we could both get some sleep before work. My head was hurting thinking about Sheila and Anthony. Seein' Tyrone with Samantha had made my heart ache just a bit.

"We all had hard lives. Fuck, everybody black and livin' in Tuskegee has it hard. Delilah has always been off. From the moment her daddy got locked up for molestin' her and her momma blamed her for takin' her man away from her, Delilah been bat shit crazy. But she came from crazy ass stock and the nut don't fall too far from the tree." Tre laughed at his own joke.

Tre took his clothes off and climbed onto the bed, patting the covers for me to join him. I sighed knowing he wanted sex. He always wanted sex but still had the energy to fuck his three or four side hoes, too.

"Tre, I'm tired," I said, hoping he'd let me off the hook.

"Well, let me put you to bed, then," he smiled, rubbing his dick.

I looked at him. His chocolate skin and grey eyes were so opposite. He was a mutt, like my momma used to say. The Creole in his family coming out in his curly black hair that he kept in a low 'fro, and his eyes that changed from blue to grey depending on his mood. His long, pointed nose and small mouth showed his white lineage. His small teeth, the front one chipped by Tyrone, were only visible on rare occasions. But he was definitely black below the waist. He hung a good nine inches with a regular erection, gaining an extra inch or two when he had a serious hard-on.

He'd ruined me. I thought I was stuck with him and would never find anyone else that could fit me until... Tyrone. I smiled at that thought suddenly becoming aroused. Tre would have to do since Ty was tied down now. I bent over and grabbed my ankles and Tre hopped out of the bed to indulge. I fantasized about the way Ty had bent me over and taken me his first night out of prison.

I had to bite my bottom lip not to call out Ty's name as Tre drilled me, or whoever he fantasized me to be this time.

# Tyrone

It felt good to be home. I wanted to shower and take a nap. I took my shoes off at the door and headed straight for the bedroom. I was happy Sam was there with me. We'd taken our vacation together, and just in time. I would have hated to have had to explain what I had gotten locked up for.

For the next thirty days, Sam and I were going to enjoy just being together. I kinda felt bad because she was leaving her children at home but their dad was there. And we had planned a week-long trip to Orlando with them so that I could get to know them better and they could say they did something cool during the summer. Their last day of school was this Friday, but now that Delilah was locked up and fired, I wondered what Sam would do about child care.

When I made it to the doorway of my bedroom, I smiled. She had replaced my old sheets with new ones. A red and black yin-yang comforter covered my King-sized bed, and the sheets underneath matched with little yin-yang symbols printed on them.

"They're Egyptian cotton," she advised me, "you deserve to sleep like the king that you are."

She walked up behind me and wrapped her arms around me. Her belly against my back was warm and firm. It made me smile to know I had two little people brewing in there. I turned to face her. She started to unbutton my shirt, a sly smile on her face.

"Baby, I need to take a shower. I feel nasty as hell," I confessed, wanting to wash the incarceration off my skin.

"I'm gonna join you," she said, not stopping.

She peeled my shirt off of me and started working on my pants. When she'd removed them, she left me in my boxers and undressed herself. She had on a sundress so it only took her untying the halter strands for the fabric to tumble to the floor. Her breasts sat, swollen on her chest. Her usually tight stomach stretched out a little making way for the lives that were growing in there. I hadn't noticed the change in her body until now. Thought that maybe she was picking up a little stress weight which didn't bother me because I loved every inch and every pound of her.

I stood, admiring her and considering bypassing the shower to make love to her. She blushed at me.

"I never thought you'd like me pregnant," she admitted, "that's one of the reasons I was scared to tell you."

"And the other reasons?" I coaxed.

"I needed to be sure that I was done with Kris before telling you because I knew you would want to be more than just my part-time."

"And you had to fuck him to make that determination?" I couldn't stop myself from asking.

"Ty, you just got home. Do we have to do this now?" Sam's eyes begged me to stop.

"I just need to know what I'm signing up for," I said, not stopping.

"You knew I was married when you got involved with me, Tyrone. Now you gotta problem with that? You mad 'cause I slept with my husband? I didn't know we were exclusive. I can't believe you're questioning me when word on the street is you fucked Delilah," she was so angry spit was flying from her lips.

"I didn't fuck Delilah. Bitch just sucked my dick," I explained, revealing more than I had intended to.

Sam's face was wet with tears. She stared at me in disbelief. Like me gettin' head from Delilah was any more of a betrayal than her fuckin' Anthony. I walked past her to get in the shower. I didn't care to tend to her bruised ego. I needed to bathe and rest. She could lick her own wounds and decide whether or not she wanted me or Anthony.

I wasn't a bitch nigga like him. I wasn't gonna be strung along and she needed to know that. I turned the water on full blast and washed every inch of myself from my hair to the soles of my feet. Sam didn't come to join me and something in me told me she wouldn't be there when I got out.

I breathed the steam in and out, trying to calm myself. *If she's gone, her ass can stay gone,* I told myself not feeling the yo-yo game she was playing. I'd seen her look back at Anthony before she got into the car at the courthouse. I knew she wasn't done with him. It just wasn't that simple. They had years together. They had children together. But none of this was my problem.

"I'm not Nel," I spoke into the steam.

"No, you're not," Sam's voice echoed through the fog.

I had no idea when she'd come into the bathroom or how long she'd been in there. I pulled the curtain back. She was sitting on the toilet with her head in her hands.

"I thought you would have been halfway to Halcyon by now," I admitted.

"I'm not Kris," Sam said, her eyes shooting daggers at me.

"I didn't say you were," I retorted.

"But you expected me to leave you like he does your sister."

"Honestly, Sam, I don't know what to expect," I said, pulling the curtain closed.

She was right, though. *I can't even shower in peace,* I thought, the tension returning to my neck and shoulders. I rested my palms against the tile. I knew I was just tired and didn't want to say anything I didn't mean.

"She's my sister, baby," Sam spoke into the silence.

I didn't respond. I had no idea who she was talking about and hated when women started their stories in the middle.

"My momma told me before she died. Told me about my father and how he had another family 'cross town. He'd been payin' her shush money and put us up in one of the houses he owned so she didn't have to pay rent. Gave it to her as a gift the day I was born, the deed was in her name. She never spent a penny he gave her. Worked hard as hell as a maid to provide for me. Paid my way through college and everything."

Sam was spilling her past into the atmosphere like a secret she'd held onto for too long. I turned off the water and pulled the curtain open again. I felt like what she was saying was important. But I still had no idea who the *she* was that Sam was talking about. She handed me the towel from the rack. I dried off as she continued.

"Over $250,000 in sixteen years. 'Til he got locked up. I always assumed it was for dealin' or somethin'. She'd set up an account and just let it build interest."

"Over a quarter mil?" I asked, baffled.

"Yeah," Sam said her face showing her disgust, "and since her passing, I've invested it and flipped it to five times that. But I waste it because it pisses me off that my momma was kept in the shadows her whole life."

I cleared my throat waiting for her to continue.

"But she loved him. Was never with another man 'til the day she died. She wasted her life hoping he'd leave his family and come be with her. Then, when he got locked up, the hopelessness of ever being his main chick ate away at her 'til she was nothing. Some call it cancer, I call it loss of hope," Sam started to tear up.

"Damn," was the only response I could muster. I felt bad for Sam. *We've all had fucked up lives,* I thought.

"Then that psycho bitch killed her momma. Burned down the house with the poor woman asleep in it. They say when the police asked her why she did it, she said because her momma slept with her man, like it was a valid reason." Sam's eyes were glued to the floor.

I still didn't know who she was talking about but I hoped it wasn't Tammy. They were both from Tuskegee. I tried to remain patient so that she wouldn't stop sharing with me.

"I thought hiring her was a way to get to know her. To give this woman back something because she lost her daddy, her momma, and her sanity all in the same year. But she's a bad seed, baby. Somethin' ain't right wit' her."

Sam paused again. She looked up at me then back at the floor when she saw the light bulb come on for me.

"*Delilah is your sister?*" I asked, thrown all the way off. I felt my knees buckle and my head start to spin. I could only imagine what Sam felt.

"Yes," she said, tears finally falling down her cheeks.

"Oh baby," I said, stepping out of the tub, my towel wrapped around my waist.

"So if you've slept with her, I can't be with you. Finding out about her and Kris was the nail in the coffin for me and him," she sobbed.

"Does he *know* she's your sister?" I asked.

"No," she responded.

"Does *she* know?" I asked.

"I don't think so but I didn't get the chance to find out," she explained her plan.

"Damn," I said, again, rubbing her back as she soaked my bathroom floor with her tears.

I opened the door to the bathroom. The steam billowed out.

"Come on, let's lay down. We both need rest and," I paused, extending my hand to her, "it sounds like you've got a lot to get off your chest."

Sam took my hand and I led her into the bedroom. Her bag was open on the dresser. She had been preparing to leave. *But she stayed*, I smiled to myself.

We sat on the foot of the bed and I let her cry until she was tired of crying. I knew the kinda pain family could cause and that she needed to get all of that hurt and pain out so there would be room for our little ones to grow in there. It was strange to me that in all those years with Anthony she had never felt comfortable enough to share this with him. She was allowing herself to be vulnerable with me and that was a huge thing. Maybe, one day soon, I'd open up to her and show her all of me. But not just yet. She still had some loose ends to tie up and, honestly so do I.

# Sheila

Anthony and I went to breakfast at the Egg & I. It was our favorite little hideaway. He was being so sweet, rushing to open every door, pulling out my chair. His actions were caring and gentle. All it took was a cancer diagnosis, Delilah going to jail, and Sam leaving him for my brother to make me the priority. That left a sour taste in my mouth.

"So, how are you feeling?" He asked, patronizing me.

I rolled my eyes and prepared to read his ass the riot act. My phone rang.

"Sheila Price," I answered, cheerily. "Yes, I can come in this afternoon. Ok. Thank you."

I hung up the phone and my face hung to the floor with it. I sipped my water and reviewed the menu. All of a sudden, I wasn't hungry. Anthony stared at me, waiting for me to say something.

"That was the Cancer Center. They want me to come in so they can run tests this afternoon," I explained.

"Want me to go with you?" He asked, reaching for my hand.

I softened. I hadn't told anyone else that I had cancer so him being there would be great for my nerves. Him even asking to be there made me smile. He could have left me to fend for myself.

"That would be nice," I said, squeezing his hand. "You know I really don't get you. You cheat on your wife with me, cheat on me with Delilah, cause all kinds of chaos, but then there's this other side of you. The loving side. The side that I see when you hold me and do shit like offer to come to the Cancer Center with me. But," I paused, my face getting hot, "I couldn't get you on the phone when I was at the doctor's office, seeing about *our* child."

"Bae, I'm sorry. I'm so sorry," he pled. "Are you still..." He asked, interrupted by the server who took our orders, collected our menus, and walked away.

"No, Anthony. I had an abortion."

His eyes filled with tears. He sniffled a few times, trying to compose himself.

"It's my fault," he said, accepting responsibility for my actions. "If I had been there for you, maybe our baby would still be alive."

Anthony hung his head. I almost felt bad about making such a rash decision. Sam hadn't aborted her child, even with all that was going on in her life. I sat now, regretting the decision I had made. Then another thought came to mind. I needed some confirmation from Anthony about Sam.

"Is there a chance that Sam's baby is yours?" I asked the burning question.

"No, Bae," he sighed, seemingly upset by the reality. "Those babies are all Tyrone."

"*Babies,*" I got excited. Ty hadn't told me that Sam was pregnant with twins.

"So, are you done with Sam?" I asked, needing to know.

"Bae, I honestly don't know," he confessed, being honest for what was probably the first time since I'd met him.

"Wait... what?" I asked, feeling my blood start to boil.

"She's been fuckin' around on me. Lyin' to me and now she's about to have two babies by another nigga. Not one... but two."

The server brought out our food but I definitely didn't have an appetite now. I was furious at how hypocritical Anthony was being. Not because I wanted him to be with his wife and not me, but because he had the *nerve* to feel a way about her doing exactly what he had been doing to her for over a decade now. The only difference was she left his ass for Ty. *That's what's really fuckin' with him. The fact that she did what he never thought she'd do: she moved on,* I thought to myself. I stirred in my food before looking up at him with lasers shooting from my eyes.

"Which one you wanna be: the pot or the kettle?" I asked, letting the meaning sink in.

Anthony scoffed at me calling him on his shit. His ego was definitely bruised. I smiled. I was starting to like Sam more and more. She had this nigga's number and wasn't even trying to. She was just making the best decision for her based on the situation he'd put her in.

Anthony ate his food, refusing to talk to me. His feelings were hurt and I could tell. He wasn't done with Sam. He'd just told me so. If I stayed with him, I had to worry about his stupid ass running up behind her and possibly trying to do somethin' to my brother. I wasn't havin' that. For the first time in my life I chose to stop some shit I saw coming from happening.

I got up from my seat and started walking towards the door. I heard Anthony call my name but didn't look back. I picked up the pace in case he'd gotten up to follow me. By the time I got to my car, I was almost running. Running *away* from the pain. Away from the bullshit. I got in my Cavalier and sped off to the only place I knew Anthony wouldn't come lookin' for me.

# Samantha

I was sound asleep in Ty's arms when I heard heavy, frantic knocks on the front door. I slipped from underneath his arm and the warmth of his body, making sure not to wake him and walked to the door. I looked through the peephole and saw Sheila standing there. She was lookin' over her shoulder like the Boogie Man was after her. I pulled the door open before she woke Tyrone up with her knocking.

"Sheila, Ty's sleep," I said, in a hushed tone. "Everything ok?"

"No, it's not," Sheila said, out of breath. "I just need to hide out here for a lil' while."

"The cops after you or somethin'," I asked, furrowing my brow. My body blocked her entrance to the apartment. Sister or not, she wasn't bringin' anymore shit into Ty's life.

"No," Sheila laughed, realizing how she must have looked to me. "I just need to get away from Anthony for a while and I know he won't come lookin' for me over here," she explained.

"Oh, now *that* I can relate to," I said, laughing.

I let her into the house. She took off her shoes and placed them by the door. She walked over to the couch and sat down heavily. I knew she wanted to talk. I kinda wanted to, too. But first I had to pee. Two babies on my bladder were way worse than one. I made a beeline for the bathroom.

After I relieved myself and washed my hands, I prepared myself to go back into the living room and to talk to my husband's pregnant mistress. *Think of it as talking to your boyfriend's sister*, I tried to convince myself but it wasn't working. There was a knot in the pit of my stomach and it wasn't the twins.

"I know I'm probably the last person on Earth you want to talk to," Sheila started when I walked back into the living room.

I nodded in agreement, "You're right about that. But I really do feel like we *need* to talk," I admitted.

"Let me start by saying I..."

"I know you didn't know Kris was married. I've known him for a long time. I know how he lies and manipulates feelings," I cut her off.

"I still want to apologize," Sheila said earnestly.

"I need to be apologizing to you," I responded.

"For what?" Sheila asked, baffled.

"For the next week, months... hell, years that you're gonna be trapped in that man's web. It's not a pleasant place to be. He slowly sucks the life out of you. He's an incubus. A master manipulator who convinces you that your sole existence is to vie for his approval. And he can convince you that you are his and only his while he's got another woman hiding under the bed."

"Or in the closet," Sheila chimed in, trying to lighten the mood.

We shared a laugh. Her phone started vibrating. I looked at it, then at her. She wanted to answer it. *Poor thing. Her nose is wide open*, I thought feeling sorry for her.

Sheila took a deep breath and pressed the power button. I smiled knowing that it took every bit of will power she had in her.

"So, you're having twins?" She asked turning the conversation to me.

She looked longingly at my stomach. There was so much hurt in her expression.

"Yeah, we heard two heartbeats the other day," I gushed, trying to perk up the mood, "I never wanted to have one child. Now I'm about to have 5, and two at one time."

Sheila forced a smile. She was having a hard time keeping her emotions in check.

"How far along are you? Have you... y'all heard the heartbeat yet?" I asked hoping that talking about her pregnancy would cheer her up.

"No, I didn't get to hear its heartbeat. Anthony never came with me to the doctor, and I was only a few weeks along," she said, never looking me in the eyes.

*Was? Did she just say was?* I asked myself.

"Was?" I asked aloud my heart ripping open.

"Yeah," she said softly. "I had an abortion on Friday."

"Did Kris make you get the abortion?" I asked, becoming furious.

"No. No!" She defended him. "He's actually all torn up because I had one. But... well... it's a long story," she said, dismissing the entire topic.

"It's ok. I've got time," I coaxed. I couldn't tell if it was curiosity fueling my interest in what had happened or my genuine concern for her.

"Can I ask you something, Sam," Sheila asked, her face becoming stern. She looked me directly in the eyes.

"Yeah, ask away," I invited.

"Are you serious about being with my brother? Because Anthony admitted to me that he's not done with you and," she paused thinking of the best way to express her thoughts, "Tyrone has never been loved back the right way, ya know. From his dad abandoning him and our mom to my dad leaving, too. Then our momma bein' what she was...," she paused again. This time she let out a heavy sigh.

"Look," Sheila said, her voice shaking. "My brother has had a hard life. There are things he doesn't think I know about that I do. He's always protected me. I mean, he just went to jail this weekend protectin' my stupid ass. And I know I may be so outta line comin' in here questionin' you, but Ty's all I got and I would really like it if he could be happy for once."

Her eyes filled with tears. I reached out and touched her shoulder. "Sheila, I've been with Tyrone for a year almost. And yes, I've been married the whole time but he knew that. What started out as friendship has developed into something so beautiful it multiplied into two babies. I sometimes wonder what my life would have been like if I'd waited 'til I met Ty instead of settling for Kris' triflin' ass."

"But everything happens in perfect time," Sheila added.

"Right," I agreed, "and I probably wouldn't have appreciated Ty back then."

"Sam, Ty wasn't this man back then," she said, laughing. "He's grown a lot. Trust me. I'm honestly shocked that he hasn't killed Anthony yet."

"He's been holding back because of me," I confessed, "Kris, as fucked up a person as he is, is still my husband and the father of my children. Ty knows that hurting him would hurt me and the kids."

"Hmmmm," Sheila said, thoughtfully, "you really *are* good for him. I'm so happy you two found each other. Regardless of the circumstances!"

"Me, too. And it's not all one-sided. Ty has been great for my self-esteem. He's shown me that a woman can be treated well. My whole life, I watched my momma wait for my daddy to leave his wife. It leaves a bad taste in your mouth, ya know."

I felt myself opening up. Sheila had a very non-judgmental nature. You felt like you could tell her all your secrets and she'd love you anyway. Maybe it was her eyes. She and Ty both had the same eyes. They were so kind. I wondered if they were their mother's. I knew so little about her. About any of their past. And there was so much I wanted to know. Like the reason that Ty had nightmares and would wake-up sweaty and panting. I knew he wasn't gonna open up to me about it. At least not anytime soon. Maybe Sheila could give me some insight since we were in "friend mode".

"We would have been cool under different circumstances," Sheila said giving me the first genuine smile I'd seen since she got here.

"Yeah, I'd like to think so," I said sharing her smile. "There's no reason we can't form a friendship now," I offered.

"Other than the fact that I'm fuckin' your husband," Sheila admitted.

"Yeah," I said, "There's that."

We both laughed at our circumstances. I'm sure she was just as delighted by the fact that Kris would lose his mind if he found out we were friends. Tyrone came around the corner. In all of our talking and laughing we'd forgotten to be quiet.

"Look at my girls gettin' along," he said, walking over and sitting on the arm of the couch. He leaned down and kissed me on the forehead.

"Yeah," I said between giggles, "I think we've bonded over our bad taste in men." I laughed again then looked up at him. He faked being offended.

"Not you, Ty," Sheila said to him.

"I know," he laughed, "and I don't care if you were talkin' 'bout me. I'm just happy I didn't come in here to find y'all tryna kill each other."

"I think the fight's over. I'm right where I wanna be and I think Sheila is on her way out of Hurricane Kris's destructive path," I said leaning back into him.

"Yeah," Sheila agreed. "I think I'd better get outta that situation while I've still got my life."

But there was something in her tone, something in her eyes that told me that she would be back with Kris before the sunset.

# Anthony

Sheila's phone kept going to voicemail. I was getting frustrated. Between her and Sam, I had about had enough of being ignored and disrespected. Delilah was locked up so I couldn't call her. I sat at the table and ate my breakfast, planning my next move. Tyrone wasn't takin' my wife away from me, pregnant or not. And I wasn't lettin' Sheila go, either. I was gonna make that nigga watch while I fed his babies *and* kept fuckin' his sister. *Who the fuck he think I am,* I thought, angrily.

I paid my check and called my brother-in-law, Matt, to come pick me up since Sheila had left me stranded when she threw her tantrum. I stood outside smokin' a square tryin' to calm my nerves. These hoes had me fucked up. But I'm gonna show 'em just who they're fuckin' with.

Matt pulled up in the work truck. When I got in he gave me a look before pulling off.

"Where's your car?" he asked, a smirk on his face.

"It's at Sheila's house," I said, annoyed.

"Ya know, I should charge yo' ass for this pick-up," he joked.

"Go 'head and I'll tell Andrea about the stripper you been financin' for the past 3 years. When's the baby due again?"

I truly was not in the mood for his shit. We drove towards Sheila's house. He knew where it was because he'd come and picked up the work truck from there some nights when I lied to Sheila about bein' on call and was with somebody else.

A call came through while we were on our way. A woman with her keys locked in her car at Vaughn Road Park. My mind drifted to some woman who had just finished her workout or her tennis lesson sweating with tights and a sports bra on.

"It's on the way," I said, causing Matt to give me the side eye.

"Mmm hmm," he grunted but headed to the park.

When we got there, we saw a lone car in the parking lot. Everyone else was at work. We got out of the truck and I started laughing.

"Small world," Beth said her face showing as much shock at the coincidence as mine.

"Yeah, it is," I agreed, laughing a little harder.

Matt worked at unlocking the door to her Land Rover while I admired her in her sports bra and short tights.

"You lookin' for somethin'?" she asked, rolling her eyes.

"I think I found it," I said, "and you don't seem to have much of an issue with me lookin'," I pointed out the fact that she'd chosen her outfit.

"You really have no shame, do you?" Beth asked, appearing offended.

Something told me she was frontin'. She could have walked away but she was right there, letting me know that she was more intrigued by me than she was lettin' on.

"Fuck!" Matt cursed loudly. He hated unlocking vehicles.

"Need some help, Bruh?" I asked my eyes never leaving Beth.

"Naw, I got it, man," he said his ego gettin' in the way of me helping. "You know I just hate doin' this shit," he admitted.

I walked towards Beth. She took a couple of steps back, but that didn't stop me. *She playin' coy*, I told myself. I had my sights set on her and I was gonna have her.

"I want you," I said flashing a confident smile.

"Does that shit really work on these hetero-hoes you got fightin' over you and shit?" Beth asked, frowning.

I just smiled. That was her way of letting me know she was gay. *As long as she got a pussy there's a potential to fuck*, I laughed to myself. She didn't know it but she was as good as fucked.

"Look," Beth said getting frustrated, "I gotta go pack up Delilah's stuff so it don't end up on the curb while she's servin' time. Told her to leave yo' ass alone."

"She jumped on Sheila all by herself. All in that woman's house and shit," I corrected her.

"Three sides to every story: her side, your side, and the truth," she said sarcastically. "All I know is your ass is out here, free and clear, and my woman is locked up for three months."

*Her woman, she really didn't know Delilah, did she?*

"Got it," Matt said opening the door to Beth's SUV.

She stomped away, walking up to Matt and handing him a check. She got in her truck and slammed the door. Matt jumped out of the way as she peeled out of the parking lot.

"You sure gotta way with the ladies' man," he laughed. "You almost gotta brotha run down and shit."

"Mmm hmmm," I said, not paying him any attention.

I wasn't done with her, either. There's somethin' about havin' to chase a woman that got me goin'.

*****

Matt dropped me off and I headed to Delilah's. Beth had pretty much invited me over there.

"I might as well help her move the stuff," I said to myself, acknowledging that I was partially responsible for Delilah being in jail. I parked in the back of Delilah's duplex and went in the back door. Beth was bent over a box putting things from the nightstand inside of it. She as muttering something under her breath.

"I see you've found Pandora's Box," I said watching from the doorway.

Beth jumped and turned around, apparently startled to hear a male voice in the house. She looked at me with fire in her eyes.

"I don't bite," I said.

"I beg to differ," she said rolling her eyes.

"Well, if you like to be bitten...," I flirted.

"What do you want, Kristopher?" She asked like a mother scorning her child.

"I wanted to come help pack. I figured you'd need the help," I answered. *And to get some of you*, I stated my true intentions to myself.

"Depends on the kinda help you're offerin'," she said unable to hide her smile.

*I'm in there*, I thought knowing I had just gotten the green light.

I walked across the room, getting so close to her that she stumbled backwards, her body pushing the drawer closed.

"What kinda help are you willin' to accept?" I asked. "Your *woman* is locked up for ninety days. I'm sure you got an itch that's gonna need to be scratched."

"You can't scratch no itch I got," she said curtly.

"Wanna bet," I challenged her, my lips almost touching hers.

I slid my hand onto her ass and squeezed, excited that it was really as soft as it looked. She didn't push me back. There was a curiosity in her face. She wanted to find out what all the hype was about. I didn't give her the chance to change her mind. I kissed her passionately. I wondered if she'd ever been with a man. The thought made my dick so hard it hurt. I was gonna take my time with her. I kissed her, sliding my tongue down her neck, taking each of her freckled breasts into my mouth. I nibbled on her bubble gum pink nipples.

She sighed, enjoying my touch. She grabbed my pecs and squeezed them, giggled when I made them jump. Her hand slid into my pants, pausing when she felt my hardness. She just left it resting on top of it, as if she was unsure what to do with it.

"I've never been..." she said, sighing a confession, her mouth on my ear as I sucked her neck. I was enjoying how quickly she marked up, leaving a trail of love marks all over her neck and breasts. "I've never been with a man," she finally got out.

*I knew it*, I laughed to myself, *I'm 'bout to break her in.*

"I'll go slow," I promised in between kisses.

I let go of her ass to pull down her tights. I shifted our bodies until we were on the bed. Kneeling down, I went to work on her hairless pink pussy. Just like I had in the same spot so many times with Delilah. I gave her the best head I had given in my life. Beth squealed and squirmed. Grabbed my head, then the covers. Her legs trembled in ecstasy. She came over and over, convulsing, trying to inch away, tapping out on the bed.

When I was ready and knew she was wet enough for me to slide in, I started stretching her as I sucked on her clit.

One finger. Then two. Three was the max she could take. I spread them apart, little by little to open her up. She was so tight. So wet. Her skin was flushed red. I fingered her until she begged to feel me.

I got up and began to undress. She sat up on her elbows and watched, putting one of Delilah's vibrators against her clit. Her eyes got big when I pulled my pants and boxer briefs down and my one-eyed monster was staring back at her. I massaged myself, watching her make herself cum over and over in front of me.

I eased into the bed, climbing on top of her and kissing her. I guided myself into her inch-by-inch. She gasped into my mouth, writhing beneath my weight. She bit my bottom lip when I got my full self inside of her. I stroked. She hollered. I introduced her to the full experience of being with a man. Puttin' her legs up on my shoulders. Bent her over, watching her round, pink ass shiver and ripple as I entered and exited her.

She started to move *with* me. Her pussy squeezed my dick so tight I had to distract myself to keep from nuttin' quick. I alternated between fuckin' her and givin' her head. I watched her eyes roll back in her head. Watched her face morph into different stages of pleasure and pain. I was experiencing the best ego stroke ever.

*Fuck Sam. Fuck Sheila. Hell, fuck Delilah*, I thought to myself as I neared climax. I just wanted this.

"BETH!" I grunted, spraying myself into her.

We lay there gasping for air, the midday sun shining into the room. We'd get the house packed up later. Beth seemed to share my sentiment. She rolled on top of me, easing herself down onto me. She rode me, awkwardly at first, but finally found her rhythm. It was my turn to moan and scream. I was her tool for pleasure. She held herself up with her hands pressed against my chest. Her nails dug into my skin. I lay there letting Beth indulge herself. I enjoyed every stroke. I grabbed her ass and held on for dear life. We fucked until we were tired. She fell asleep in my arms her head rested on my chest. She'd restored my confidence in my manhood.

# Sheila

I felt bad lying to Tyrone but I decided not to tell him the reason I had to leave. I drove to the Cancer Center smiling. Sam was a good woman and she and Ty fit together so well that it made *me* blush. I just hoped she kept her word and moved forward with the divorce. Anthony was relentless when he set his sights on somethin' and I had a feeling things were gonna get way worse before they got better with this situation.

I pulled into the parking lot and got out to walk into the building. I was a ball of nerves. I wished someone could have been here with me, but the doctor said it was caught early so there was no point in worrying everyone about nothin'. I had a seat in the waiting area, a pile of paperwork sitting in my lap on a clipboard. When it asked about recent surgeries, I stopped. *I wonder if the abortion counts*, I thought to myself. I decided to ask.

Walking up to the Receptionist's window, I leaned forward whispering like I was embarrassed.

"Excuse me, but do D&C's count as recent surgeries?"

"Yes, ma'am," the Receptionist said matching my tone, "and make sure to put the kind of surgery and the date that you had it done in the spaces to the right."

"Thank you," I said, turning and walking back to my seat.

I completed the paperwork, taking it back to the Receptionist desk and sat back down to wait. It seemed like a forever passed before they called me back. I was weighed, had blood drawn, and my blood pressure was checked before I was led to a room to wait on the Doctor. The waiting was the part that killed me. I just wanted to get this over with.

I checked my phone, realizing that it was the sixth time that I had done that since I'd gotten there. Still nothing from Anthony. My heart sank. I wondered what, or who, he was doing. He hadn't hit me up since I'd turned my phone off when I was at Ty's house. He hadn't even left a voice message. I started feeling stupid because I'd left him at the restaurant and ignored his call. Just when I was about to send him a text, the door opened and the doctor walked in. *I hear you, God*, I said in my head taking that as my sign to leave Anthony wherever the hell he was.

"Ms. Price," he said, holding my chart.

"Yes," I answered my voice shaking.

"I'm Doctor Kingston. How are you feeling?"

"Fine. Kinda nervous. Trying to digest all of this," I admitted.

"I can understand," he sympathized. "A cancer diagnosis has a way of rattling a person."

"Indeed," I agreed.

"Unfortunately Ms. Price, we won't be able to do a Pap Smear today," he said reading my chart.

"Because of the abortion?" I asked, my head hanging.

"Yes. Your body needs to heal before we begin taking samples and," he looked at the information in my chart again, "your D&C was less than 3 days ago."

"I know," I said sadly, my eyes glued to the floor.

"But the results we received from your Obstetrician revealed some cancerous tissue, so we do want to start you on a few medications that will keep the cancer at bay until we can run the additional tests, ok," he told me looking up to make sure that I understood and was in agreement.

I nodded yes. He pulled a prescription pad out of the front pocket of his lab coat and scribbled some indiscernible writing onto the paper. Handing it to me, he got up to leave.

"I'd like to see you back in 4 weeks, ok," he said more as a request than a demand. "Please follow-up with your Gynecologist to make sure you heal properly from the D&C," he urged, his face full of concern.

"I will," I croaked out embarrassment filling my eyes.

I walked back towards the front stopping by the Receptionist's desk to pay my deductible and schedule my next appointment. Everything was muffled and blurry as I left the Cancer Center. The sun shone and was blinding, it hurt my eyes. I wanted to cry but didn't have the strength to. I felt terrible and knew that my emotions had taken their toll on my body. I decided to go home and take a nap. I'd sort through all of this shit when I woke up.

*****

When I got home, Anthony's car was gone. I figured he'd gotten Matt to come get him and bring him to the house to get his car. *Maybe he got one of his hoes to bring him,* I thought to myself, getting angry then being overcome with sadness. I dragged myself out of my car and into my house. My empty house. *I need a dog or a cat or something,* I thought, *there's no life in this damn house when Jeff wasn't here.*

I plopped down onto the couch and set my alarm to get Jeff from school. Before I sat my phone on the table, I checked it one last time for any calls or messages. Still nothing.

I covered my head with one of my throw pillows and cried myself to sleep.

# Tyrone

Nel rushed out of here with a lie about having a meeting. I didn't press the issue because I figured she didn't want to admit to me or Sam that she was leaving to run up behind Anthony's no good ass. Not too long after that, Sam had gotten dressed and claimed to have another meeting with her attorney. That didn't sit well with me, either. I picked up my phone and made a call.

"Hello?" she answered, sleep in her voice.

"Can you get away?"

"Sure," she said clearing her throat.

I heard groaning in the background and knew she and her old man had been sleeping.

"Is this a bad time?" I asked, really wanting to see her but knowing that dude put his hands on her.

"No, it's not," she said quietly.

"Ok. Meet me at the spot in half an hour?" I asked.

"Yeah, Sheila, I'll be there in a few," she agreed. "Love you."

"I love you, too," I said, meaning every word.

We hung up the phone and I sat at the foot of my bed smiling. In another lifetime we would have been together. But circumstances just didn't allow for that. I had to sit back and watch her being mistreated and *now* she had front row seats to me and Sam starting a family.

*The Universe has a terrible sense of humor*, I thought pulling on my jeans. The way that all of us knew one another, Sam being married to Anthony, Anthony fuckin' my sister and Delilah, and Tammy raising my nephew like he was her own son and not the product of Tre fuckin' around on her. All of it seems like some kinda reality TV show. I pulled my hair into a ponytail and grabbed my keys, heading for the door.

*****

I pulled into the parking lot of the Montgomery Museum of Fine Arts. We would leave her car there and head to the Drury Inn. I called to book our room while I waited. A few minutes after I'd hung up with the hotel, my phone rang. Her face and her number displayed on the caller ID. I smiled, figuring she was calling to apologize for making me wait. Usually she would have beat me here.

"Hello?" I answered the phone with a smile on my face.

No one said anything. The phone hung up and the hair stood up on the back of my neck. My heart raced as I cranked up the car and threw it into gear. My tires peeled as I sped out of the parking lot.

# Tammy

"Where the hell you goin'?" Tre asked, half-asleep.

"Sheila just called. She's not dealing with everything that's happened well and needs to talk," I lied.

"You shole are involved in this whole mess," he said sitting up on his elbows. "Sheila's drama ain't your problem."

"As long as she's Jeff's momma, her *life* is my problem. Should be *yours*, too," I pointed out.

"Whatever," he scoffed, rolling over and turning his back to me, "don't make that running to her rescue shit a habit like you used to for Delilah. You see where she ended up."

That hurt but I didn't say anything else. I was in a hurry. Something was wrong with Tyrone. I could tell he needed to talk. And I wanted see him anyway. I went to get into the shower and washed the scent of Tre off of my body.

Not too long after I'd gotten into the shower, I heard him come into the bathroom and lift the seat to the toilet. Hearing water hitting water, I turned my back to the showerhead, rinsing the soap off of my body. I put my head into the stream, wetting it so that it would be curly like Ty liked it. I heard Tre flush the commode. I hoped that he would take his ass back to sleep and not hold me up from leaving.

He left the bathroom and I sighed in relief. I hadn't realized that I had been holding my breath. I was always so tense around Tre because anything, or nothing, could set him off. I heard him come back into the bathroom.

"Forgot to wash your hands?" I asked hoping that he wasn't coming to take a shower with me.

My eyes were closed, water flowing down my face, so I didn't see the belt come into the shower. Tre saying nothing made me tense up again and, just as I opened my eyes to see if he was still in the bathroom, I felt leather tighten around my neck. Tre snatched me back, making me slip in the tub.

I grabbed at the belt around my throat, my feet slipping on the slick tub. Tre snatched me up and out of the tub, slamming me onto the bathroom floor.

"You're a lyin' bitch!" he yelled, never releasing the pressure from the belt.

I couldn't speak and couldn't figure out what I'd lied about now. *My phone*, I thought, realizing I'd left it on the dresser. I felt myself starting to black out. He was really going to kill me this time. *Tyrone is worth dying for*, I thought before drifting into the darkness.

# Sheila

My phone rang. I jumped up to answer it, hoping it was Anthony.

"Nel!" Tyrone said frantically when I answered the phone.

"Ty?" I said shaken by the urgency in his voice.

"Yeah, it's me. Look, you gotta get to Tammy and Tre's house. I don't have time to explain, just call the cops and meet me there. You gotta key, right?" he asked.

"Yeah, Jeff's key should be here. I'll be there in a few."

"Ok," he said hanging up the phone before I could ask any questions.

The way he ended the call lit a fire under me. I jumped up completely forgetting about my pity party, and ran into Jeff's room looking for his key. It was times like these that made me grateful that my child was borderline OCD. The key hung on a nail that he'd put into the wall just behind his door. I grabbed it and ran like my life depended on it to my car. I don't even know if I locked the door to my house.

I dialed 911 on the way down the Southern Boulevard and gave them Tre and Tammy's address. Assuming that it was the usual, I told them that there was a domestic disturbance and a woman was being abused by her husband. The operator said that she would send officers to the apartment. I sped to the Southside of Montgomery.

Even though they made bank, Tre was determined to stay on this side of town. I shook my head as I turned down Narrow Lane Road towards Red Lion Apartments. *This nigga sellin' dope*, I told myself knowing that was the reason he was so adamant about staying in the 'hood. That's where his clientele was. Tre hadn't changed at all. But I wondered what Tyrone had to do with the whole situation.

Parking in front of the building, I saw Tyrone pacing the sidewalk. He was smoking a cigarette. I was sure it was his second or third. His eyes were fixated on the door to Tre and Tammy's apartment. I knew, because of the area, that the cops were gonna take their time getting there. I felt uneasy about opening the door to their home. I knew he beat on her but I also knew that she stayed. Even worse, I knew that we lived in a state where you could use lethal force on trespassers legally, so walking into their crib wasn't a wise move.

"What's goin' on, Ty?" I asked getting out of the car.

"Just open the door, Nel," he commanded, his face balled up.

"Maybe we should wait for the cops," I suggested.

"She may be dead by then," he countered taking the key out of my hand.

I leapt in front of him, blocking the door. I heard Tre screaming and cursing at Tammy from the inside. Something in me hoped that Tammy had locked herself in a room and he was yelling at her from the other side of the door.

"Give me the key, Ty," I begged. "I have more of a reason to be here than you do. I don't want you to get hurt."

"That nigga ain't gone move *shit*," Ty said seething. "He'll jump on a woman but won't lay a hand on a damn man."

"Ty, you *just* got outta jail," I reminded him. "Please, let me go in first."

Tyrone stood there staring at me. He was so angry he wasn't thinking clearly.

"Fine," he said, thrusting his hand into my face with the key dangling from his index finger.

"Thank you," I said, softening my eyes and placing my hand on my brother's chest to calm him like I used to when we were kids. I turned around and put the key in the lock, opening the door.

"Stay here," I looked over my shoulder at Tyrone.

I walked into the house just as Tre was dragging an unconscious, naked Tammy out of the bathroom, a belt wrapped tightly around her neck.

"Tre!" I screamed making him look up at me. His eyes were wild with anger and I knew he'd lost his senses.

He dropped Tammy onto the floor and started towards me.

"The fuck you doin' here?" he asked, spit foaming in the corners of his mouth like a rabid dog.

"I was waiting for Tammy to come to the house and got worried when she didn't show," I lied.

"Bitch, you lyin'!" he spat coming within inches of my face. "I know she was talkin' to a nigga on the phone 'cause he answered when I called the number back."

"That was my brother, Tyrone. He answered my phone for me 'cause I was in the bathroom. Come on, Tre. You know Tammy ain't stuttin' nobody but you," I reasoned.

"So, you got her comin' to yo' crib to meet up wit' yo' brotha?" he asked, hearing only part of what I'd said.

"Tre, calm down. That's not what this is at…"

He slapped me so hard I saw colors. My ears rang and, before I could open my eyes, he'd popped me again. I tasted blood and felt myself lose my balance. I was headed to the floor. I felt arms catch me and looked up to see Tyrone glaring at Tre. They stood like two pitbulls ready to rip one another's throats out. Looking past Tre, I saw Tammy move. She was coming to and beginning to sit up.

"Try that shit on me you bitch ass nigga," Tyrone challenged, standing me back up on my feet but never breaking eye contact with Tre.

"The fuck you doin' in my house? Don't you know muhfuckas lose their lives walkin' up in folk's houses and shit?" Tre countered, offering a warning that made my heart ache.

"Ty, let's go," I pleaded trying to get my brother to safety. "Let the police handle this shit."

"This fuck nigga ain't shit but talk, Nel," Ty said, refusing to move. "He's a woman beater. He ain't got the balls to fight a grown ass man. Besides," he laughed, "he knows I'll whoop that ass like I did when you were in high school." Tyrone mocked Tre.

The situation was getting volatile enough without the added taunting and ripping scabs off of old wounds. At this point, Tammy was sitting up against the wall, starting to lift herself up. My eyes darted back and forth from her to Tre to Tyrone. I was frightened. *Where the fuck are the cops?* I asked myself, panicking. This shit was getting ridiculous.

Tre smirked at Tyrone, a dangerous smirk that let me know something terrible was about to happen. He reached behind his back and pulled out a Glock-9, pointing it at Ty's chest. My eyes got as big as my head. I feared that my brother was about to lose his life right before my eyes.

"Noooooo!" I heard the screams in my head break through the silence, but I knew that it wasn't me.

Tammy had gotten all the way up and mustered the strength to run-limp in the direction of the altercation. Her scream startled Tre. He looked back at her lunging in his direction and turned the gun on her. He fired one shot, hitting Tammy and sending her body spinning to the left.

"Ahhhh!" she cried out falling to the ground.

Tyrone punched him in the jaw, knocking him to the ground and making him drop the gun. Ty kicked him in the face and the gun away from his reach. He looked over at Tammy, starting to walk towards her.

"No, Ty," I screamed grabbing his arm. I finally heard sirens. "Get outta here. I can't see you in cuffs again," I begged.

"But... Tammy," he began to argue.

"I'll make sure she's ok. Just go!" I urged my brother.

Tyrone looked down at Tre who was groaning on the floor, trying to get to the gun. He stomped his hand so hard Tre hollered out in pain then kicked him in the face one more time before looking at me then back at Tammy lying motionless on the floor. He turned and walked, calmly out the door. He went the back way and I realized that he hadn't parked in front of the building. My mind was riddled with questions. I'd get the answers out of my brother later.

I rushed over to Tammy, afraid to move her.

"Tammy," I called her name, "are you ok?"

She groaned, starting to move.

"No, don't move," I instructed, happy she was alive.

"MPD!" the police announced themselves, standing at the door.

"Come in, please," I begged, "she needs an ambulance!"

The male officer came in, stopping at Tre who was still a bit disoriented from Tyrone's kickin' the shit outta him twice and stompin' on his hand. The female officer came to Tammy's aid, radioing for an ambulance.

"What happened here?" she asked.

"My friend here, Tammy, was supposed to meet me at my house and she hadn't shown so I came looking for her. I heard some noise and opened the door..." I explained.

"You have a key?" the officer interrupted me, her eyebrows furrowed.

"Yeah, he," I said, motioning towards Tre, "is my son's father. I used my son's key because I know he tends to hit on her. I came in and he had her by the neck with a belt," I said, pointing to the bruises around Tammy's neck then at the belt on the floor in the hallway.

"Mmm hmm," the officer said as the Paramedics came into the house, "and what happened to him?" she asked trying to get a full understanding of what happened.

"He pulled a gun on me after he slapped me twice, trying to make me leave," I pulled my bottom lip down to show that it was busted and bleeding. "And Tammy rushed him. He turned and shot her and I hit him. I didn't know I could hit anyone that hard. And I kicked him when he fell because I was scared that he was gonna get up and shoot me, too. He tried to grab the gun and stomped his hand like I'd seen them do on TV," I crafted the story of what happened for the officer.

She laughed at my analogy. "You know you could have gotten yourself killed," she told me, her face becoming serious.

"Yes, ma'am, I know," I said, honestly. "But, if I hadn't come in she would certainly have been dead."

I looked over at Tammy who was getting her wounds tended. I was glad to see that Tre had hit her in her shoulder. She may not be able to work at the Kia plant anymore, but at least the injury wasn't major. She was telling the medics a similar story to mine, but with details that preceded what I had witnessed. One of the medics motioned for the officer to come over.

"Be right back," she told me walking over to them.

He whispered something to her that made her look at Tre, who was sitting there refusing to give a statement at all. Then she leaned down and Tammy told her something that made her motion to her partner.

Tre's eyes grew wide when they walked into the second bedroom, Jeff's bedroom when he stayed there. They came out with three duffle bags.

"You bitch! I shoulda killed your disloyal ass years ago!" he screamed at Tammy.

She laid her head back on the stretcher, tears streaming down her cheeks. She'd finally had enough. But I knew, just like she knew, that Tre would have to be gone for her to find the strength to leave him alone for good.

I looked at Tre and realized that I had laid with that monster. That it could have been me with the bruises around my neck and a bullet wound. I had a lot to be grateful for.

"You have the right to remain silent..." I heard the male officer read Tre his Miranda Rights. They cuffed him and led him out of the apartment.

The paramedics wheeled Tammy out on a gurney and, after taking my full statement and getting my contact information, the female officer told me I was free to leave. I headed to Baptist South to be with Tammy.

When I got to the Emergency Room they told me that she wasn't ready for visitors but that she was stable. I turned around to find Tyrone sitting in the Waiting Room with his head in his hands. *How long has he been here?* I asked myself. I thought that he had come straight there until I saw that he had changed clothes. I assumed he had my blood or Tre's blood or both on his clothes and shoes.

I walked over to him and sat down.

"So, you gonna tell me what the fuck is really goin' on?" I asked making him look up.

His eyes were bloodshot and his face was red. He'd been crying. This was unsettling to me because I couldn't remember the last time I'd seen my brother cry. He was really upset and I couldn't tell if it was more about Tammy being shot or about me making him leave us in that dangerous situation and him worrying that either of us, or both of us, could have ended up dead.

"Miss Price," the nurse called to me from her desk.

I gave Tyrone a stern look letting him know he was gonna have to tell me what the fuck was goin' on.

I walked to the desk waiting to hear some news, hoping that it wasn't bad.

"Miss Alexander can have visitors now," she said, smiling and putting my name on a name tag.

I breathed a sigh of relief before looking over my shoulder at my brother.

"That's my brother. He's worried sick. Can he visit her as well?" I asked.

"Absolutely," she smiled even broader.

I motioned for Tyrone who almost ran across the waiting room. He snatched his ID out of his wallet and handed it over. When she returned his ID and gave us our nametags, we put them on and followed her into the back. She told us what room Tammy was in before returning to her post.

Tammy lay there with her eyes closed. We entered the room quietly so that we didn't disturb her. I pulled a chair up directly beside her bed. Tyrone sat in the chair across the room from her. He would be the first thing she saw when she opened her eyes. I touched her hand gently. She opened her eyes, looking down at my hand and then up into my face and smiling at me.

But when she looked straight ahead and saw Tyrone sitting there, his face flushed and tears in his eyes, there was something else in her face. They sat staring at one another, a million words travelling across the room, without a single word being said. My eyebrows raised and I excused myself. I told them that I was going to talk to her nurse and get us all something to eat. I felt like they needed some privacy.

*What in the entire fuck?* I thought, shaking my head as I left the room. I'd never thought of Tammy and Tyrone having feelings for each other, but as I got on the elevator headed to my car to get us some real food, I realized how that wasn't as far away a notion as one may think.

# Samantha

I didn't want to lie to Tyrone but I knew that telling him I was going to the house would prompt questions that I wasn't sure I was ready to give him the answers to. I mean I love him, that wasn't a question. And I didn't want to keep any secrets but I needed to speak with Kris. I had the divorce papers drawn up and ready to be signed, but I hadn't signed them like my attorney suggested before I left his office. He also suggested that we let someone else serve him because, as he put it, even the gentlest person could become a monster in these situations. But I knew Kris. We've been together ten years. He might've yelled, might've even ripped up the paperwork, but that would be the end of it. He'd beg for forgiveness and promise to never cheat again. Yeah, I know Kris.

I prepared myself mentally for the situation because I was a sucker for Kris's charms and I knew I'd fold if I didn't remain strong. I walked into the house, surprised to find it empty. I told Kris I wanted to talk and he seemed eager to meet me. I walked through the house, going into the kids' rooms and taking in their scents. I missed them! Their hugs, kisses, stories, antics, and laughter made my days and nights interesting.

But I needed a break sometimes. Especially with the way my husband fucked around leaving me to care for them or find care for them. If it wasn't for his mom and sister, Andrea, I'd be a complete wreck.

I went into our bedroom and laid across the bed. I was exhausted and hadn't done anything to make me feel tired. I realized then that I was too damned old to be having a baby. Hell, two babies. I looked around the room of the house Kris and I had picked out together. The furniture we'd chosen, the color scheme in each room. Those were the newlywed days when he skipped work just to lay up under me. Make love to me until we were drained of all energy and had to drag ourselves out of bed to get food. I threw my arm across my eyes and racked my brain trying to remember what changed. When did it all start to fall apart?

I felt my eyes fill with tears. They ran down the corners of my face. My chest heaved and before I knew it I was in a full on cry. I felt myself get nauseous and sprang up, racing to the bathroom. I vomited violently until there was nothing left. Laying on the floor I let the cool tile soothe my warm face. I took deep breaths until my stomach settled.

"This is some bullshit," I said into the bathroom.

I immediately started to miss Tyrone. I needed to get home. I laughed to myself when I realized that I *was* home. But it wasn't my home anymore. I asked for the house and the children in the divorce. I planned to keep Ty in his apartment until we sorted things out. I'm not the type to move one man out on Friday and another one in on Saturday. I wanted Ty and I date for a while, see how he was with the children, then we could talk about merging lives. I knew he wouldn't like being away from its kids like that but it had to be done.

I pulled myself up off the floor and went to get my purse and keys. I put the envelope on the kitchen table and walked out of the house. I needed to get to Tyrone. Needed his peace. We had much to discuss.

*****

"Ty baby," I walked into the apartment and called out his name. No answer.

"Where the hell is he?" I asked the empty space, putting my purse and keys onto the end table and walking through the house.

The bathroom door was open so he wasn't in the shower. The bed was made, too, so he wasn't sleeping. I started to worry. My phone rang and I ran back to the front of the house to answer it.

"Hello?" I answered breathlessly.

"So you just come over here, drop off the fuckin' divorce papers and leave? Is that what this is coming to?" Anthony said angrily on the other end of the phone.

I rolled my eyes wishing I'd checked the caller ID before I'd answered the phone.

"You weren't there and I wasn't in the mood to sit around waiting for you while you did God knows what with God knows who," I replied.

"You talking about me while you laid up with your boyfriend pregnant with his twins?"

"Look Kris, you're in no place to judge me. This is my first extramarital relationship and you're on your... what... twentieth in ten years?" I said meeting his challenge.

"Look Sam," he said knowing he was beat at his own game, "I thought we were gonna talk about this."

"There's nothing to talk about. You're going to get a nice settlement, you'll be able to live comfortably with the spousal support. You'll be able to wine and dine your bitches without a care in the world," I said getting frustrated that there'd been no call or text from Tyrone.

"We've got a *family*, Samantha. Doesn't that *mean* anything to you?" he pleaded.

"What does it mean to you, Kris? What has it ever meant to you? You're just upset that another man is fuckin' your wife and may be raising your children," I said before driving a nail in the coffin, "this ain't about me, it's about your ego."

I hung up the phone with a huff. I checked for messages from Ty again. Nothing. I dialed his cell but it went straight to voicemail. I tried Sheila's phone out of desperation. She answered on the third ring.

"Hey, you talk to Ty?" I asked getting straight to the point.

"Hey Sam. Yeah," she answered, a hint of worry in her voice. "You okay?"

"I'm cool. Well, as cool as I can be seeing the Kris just got the divorce papers and is spazzing the hell out."

"Oh," she said, thoughtfully, "well Ty is at the hospital with Tammy. Tre shot her tonight. I just picked up Jeff and some food and I'm headed back up there now."

"Okay," I said, taking a deep breath. "Tell him to call me when you get back up there, please. I'm about to lay down."

"Will do," Sheila said ending the call.

I turned the volume up on my cell phone and walked down the hallway towards the bedroom. I lay across the bed, silencing the thoughts that were running through my mind about why Ty was at the hospital with Tammy and why Tre had shot her. I was more concerned with that than whether or not she was okay.

Something about them together just didn't sit right with me. I couldn't pinpoint why, but it definitely didn't. Call it woman's intuition.

# Tyrone

*I almost lost her,* I sat here thinking to myself. Tammy was being administered pain medication and I felt my stomach churn. I'd fallen in love with Tammy from the moment I laid eyes on her. She'd been sitting in the courtroom beside Tre after I kicked his ass for fuckin' my little sister and knocking her up. Even though I could tell she was embarrassed and he'd broken her, she still had the softest hazel eyes I had ever seen.

She stood by a nigga, and by Nel after I got locked up. When she came to see me alone that first time, I was hooked. She sat across the table from me, a woman who had been writing the letters and poetry for years, and smiled a smile that could have melted ice. Just her smiling at me had transported me to another place, we were alone and in a hotel room, just me and her, where I could indulge all of the fantasies I'd had of her when I was alone in my cell.

She'd come back once a month updating me on the shit Nel wouldn't tell me during her visits. She encouraged me to finish school and was there to pick me up when I was released, got me a hotel room to stay in until Nel's graduation so I could surprise her, kept a nigga fed and bought me clothes. She even took me around to job interviews. It's damn near impossible not to love a woman like her. I remember the first time I realized Tre's ass was beatin' on her. She'd come to pick me up and had on sunglasses that she wouldn't take off and had attempted to hide her split lip with makeup. I wanted to kick his ass again. She'd begged me not to and asked that I lay up with her that night.

She'd been softer than I could've imagined and smelled like lavender and vanilla. It'd taken everything in me to practice restraint but I did because I knew too many men had come at her dick first. She needed to be handled the way a man handled a woman that he knew was invaluable. The way she'd melted into me that night, and every night we could steal way since, proved that she'd appreciated it.

When the nurses got ready to leave, I got up from my seat and walked over to the bed, sitting on the very edge of it. Tammy was dozing in and out of sleep. I was just happy she wasn't in pain. But even in her drugged drowsiness she leaned into me, resting her head in my chest, a weak smile coming across her lips. I leaned down and kissed her hair.

"I love you, woman!" I whispered, "Don't you ever leave me, I don't know what I'd do without you."

I felt my shirt get wet. She was crying. I started to panic because I wasn't trying to upset her.

"Baby, I'm sorry. Did I say something wrong?" I asked frantically.

"No," she whispered, tears leaking from her eyes. "You've just never said you loved me out loud."

I laughed at her and at myself. I knew she was emotional because she could've lost her life. Her whole world was thrown for a loop and she was gonna have to sort through it all alone when she got out of the hospital. As fucked up a person as Tre was, he was all she'd known most of her life. I felt so bad that I couldn't be there for her through this. But the reason I had gotten involved with Samantha at all was because I never expected Tammy to be available. Now she was and I was in this tangled web with Sam, Sheila, Anthony, and Delilah.

"Baby, you know I've loved you from the moment I laid eyes on you. That hasn't changed, regardless of my circumstances. And I promise to make sure you know it every day of the rest of our lives," I said tenderly wiping the tears from her cheeks.

She laughed, shifting uncomfortably.

"Now that's overkill, Ty," she said smiling.

"I mean it," I smiled, leaning down to kiss her soft lips.

She responded by sliding her tongue into my mouth. I accepted it, feeling blood flow below my waist. I placed my hand gently behind her head, my fingers tangling in the curls of her hair, and held her steady while we made out like teenagers. I wanted desperately to feel her, to taste her, but knew I needed to be gentle.

Apparently, Tammy didn't get that memo because she used her good arm and hand to reach for my dick. I was too hard to stop her. If I didn't release I was gonna end up with blue balls. She massaged me just how I liked it, swift strokes, putting pressure on my head each time her hand reached it. I always came within a matter of minutes when she worked it like that. I felt so selfish, though, because I couldn't suck on her breasts. Hell, I was afraid to touch 'em right now. Instead, I nibbled on her bottom lip between deep throat tongue thrusts and eventually eased my hand beneath the covers and under her hospital robe.

She was wet. I knew sliding inside of her would've felt like heaven right now. I eased my index finger into her, then my middle, then my ring finger. I was gentle even though I knew she liked it rough. Tonight wasn't the night to be harsh to her. I glanced down at the belt mark around her neck and the bandage on her chest and almost lost my erection. She must've noticed because she beat my dick faster and shifted her hips to get my hands to resume their motion.

"You sure," I pulled away and asked her looking directly into her eyes.

"Fuck yeah. Now hurry up before Nel or the nurses come back," she ordered, passion reddening her face.

I fingered her obediently, and the wetness on my fingers brought me closer to my own climax. She bit my lip hard when I hit her spot and tickled it with the tip of my finger. The pain inspired me to go harder until she was shuddering beneath the covers. I let out a loud cry as I came, a volcanic explosion spilling all over myself and her hand. She raised her hand to her mouth and licked it clean. That shit made my dick jump. I put myself away knowing someone, Nel or the nurses, would be paying us a visit and made a mental note to get directly in the shower when I got home.

I leaned in and kissed Tammy with all the love I had inside of me, wanting to start up again but knowing that time wasn't on our side. Her staggered breathing let me know she felt the same way I did. I lingered in her mouth, our tongues having the conversation our bodies couldn't. The longer I kissed her, the more I wished I'd waited for her. But I didn't regret my children. I didn't regret caring for Sam, but being here in this moment with Tammy let me know that what I felt for Sam wasn't love.

*Ahem!* Nel cleared her throat startling us. Both Tammy and I turned red looking like children who had gotten caught playing house.

"Am I interrupting something," she asked, a sly smirk coming across her lips. "I'm glad I let Jeff go to the gift shop to buy you a gift, Tammy. I'm sure this whole situation would have confused the hell outta my poor child."

"Knock. Knock," Nurse Debbie made her way into the room with her vitals cart and Jeff came in right behind her, holding a stuffed unicorn, four red roses, and a Get Well Soon balloon. I knew all of that probably cost him his allowance for the month. He was such a sweet kid. I'm glad Nel chose to have him. He made all of our lives better.

"Hey Uncle Ty!" he greeted me, excitedly.

"What's up, lil' man," I greeted him, dappin' him up and snatching him into a hug. He laughed and I kissed him on the head.

"Man, you gone be taller than your momma you keep growin' like you are," I laughed, shooting Nel a grin.

"That don't take much, Unc," he said laughing, "Mamma's little."

We both laughed as Nel rolled her eyes and talked to the nurse.

"Are those for me?" Tammy beamed at Jeff, interrupting us.

"Yes, Ma'am," Jeff said. "I saw them all and didn't know which one to get you so I got 'em all. I'm sorry my daddy hurt you," he said, giving her the gifts and looking towards the floor embarrassed.

"You don't have anything to be sorry for," Tammy said, softly, yet sternly. "You just promise me that you'll never lay a hand on a woman or let a woman lay her hands on you. That's not how you handle a disagreement."

"Yes, ma'am," Jeff said, still embarrassed by his father's actions.

"We're going to talk about that more a little later on," Nel said hugging her son tightly.

The nurse finished her checks and told Tammy that she should be able to leave in the next day or two. Tammy and Nel talked about Tammy staying with her once she was discharged. Tammy was all for it because she didn't want to go back to that apartment. I was excited because I'd get to see her more often and be able to help with her care. She was responsible and had short-term disability so I knew she'd be ok financially. The job would understand as long as she wasn't out too long and could return to work.

I was sure she was going to need some physical therapy and I was willing to help pay for that and help in any other way that I could, but we'd talk about all of that later. Right now having Tammy alive and free from Tre was good enough for me. I'd marry her tomorrow if I thought she'd say yes. But I had some thinking to do. Did I really want to risk what I had with Sam and my unborn children to be with Tammy? Just days ago I was excited about being a father and having Sam all to myself. What had changed? I was so caught up in my thoughts that I didn't hear Nel calling me.

She walked over and snapped her fingers in my face.

"Hey Ty," she said loudly, "Where were you just now?"

"Oh," I said, snapping back to reality, "my bad, sis. I've just gotta lot on my mind," I admitted.

"I bet you do," she laughed her know-it-all laugh, "I was trying to tell you to call Sam. She called me lookin' for you earlier. You better get in touch with her before she finds them bloody clothes and spazzes the fuck out."

"Yeah," I agreed, "I forgot all about that. Lemme call her."

"Better yet, maybe you should gone to the house. I got this here. Ma is gonna come get Jeff in a lil' while and I'mma stay the night here with Tam."

I looked at Tammy not wanting to leave her side, but she nodded, agreeing with Nel. I sighed, kissed my sister on the cheek, and dapped Jeff up again. I walked over to the side of Tammy's bed and leaned down, kissing her on the forehead. I lifted her face to mine.

"I'll be here in the morning with breakfast, ok?" I whispered.

"Ok," she said sweetly.

"I'll take a bacon, egg, and cheese biscuit with strawberry jelly and a two-pack of cinnamon raisin biscuits from Hardee's," Nel said, in true hatin' ass little sister fashion.

I cut my eyes at her and Tammy laughed. Hearing her laughter made my heart skip a beat. I turned and walked towards the door, playfully bumping into my sister on the way out. I turned at the door and looked at my family.

"I got you, Nel," I said smiling, "see y'all in the morning."

"We will. Go *home*, Ty," she laughed at my reluctance to leave, even with Sam at home and pregnant. I had a feeling they had a night full of gossip ahead once Jeff got picked up. I walked away laughing at the thought.

# Tammy

"You scandalous bitch," Sheila said, laughing loudly.

Jeff and her adoptive mom hadn't even gotten out of the hospital before she came at me, guns blazin'.

"Girl, keep yo' damn voice down before they come and run you outta here," I warned her.

"My bad," she laughed, quieting down a bit, "this is just too fuckin' good."

"What's too fuckin' good?" I asked playing innocent.

"Don't play coy with me, hoe," she said, tickled by the situation. "When did you and my brother get all cozy?"

"Years ago," I admitted deciding the cat was already out the bag so I might as well be honest. "Honestly, there was a spark in the courtroom when he got locked up for beatin' the hell outta Tre. I wrote him, first just letters of encouragement so he didn't lose his spirit like so many of our men do when they're caged. He'd write back and, I mean, his words were just so eloquent. He has a beautiful mind."

"Mmm hmm," she said stifling a giggle, "and then..." she coaxed me to keep going.

"Then Tre got the mail one day and intercepted a letter. That was the first time he beat me. I mean, he'd always put me down and cheated on me and shit. But this time he beat the holy hell outta me. Three fractured ribs over a letter. Crazy, right?" I asked reminiscing.

"Damn it, Tammy," she said, her brow creasing, "why the fuck did you stay with Tre's ass?"

"The heart wants what it wants," I said. "The only man who ever showed me any kindness was Ty. Tre threatened to kill anyone else I got involved with but I knew Ty could take him, so I fantasized about that. Ty was going to be my savior, you know?"

"I mean, I get it, but damn," Sheila said, her heart breaking right in front of me.

Her eyes welled with tears. She burst into uncontrollable sobs, her body quaking with my pain. I felt myself begin to cry, too. We cried for what seemed like an hour, letting go of all of the hurt, all the suffering we'd both endured. I cried until I was hurting. She cried until her tiny, slanted eyes were puffed almost closed. I pushed the button for my morphine pump trying to ease the pain, and she took deep breaths trying to calm herself.

We sat in silence for a while just feeling the pain that hung heavy in the room. The nurses came and checked on me after they got the alert that I'd used my pain pump. They took my blood pressure and told me to let them know if I needed anything. When they left, Sheila looked at me with tender eyes.

"So, what happened after Tre fractured your ribs?' she asked curiously.

"I tried to convince myself to stop writing Ty. That I would get myself killed, but I couldn't stop thinking about him. Not in the worried kinda way, though. I thought of him and smiled, ya know. So I got a PO Box and paid it up a year at a time. We wrote the whole time he was locked up. I wanted to see him when I would take you and Jeff up there but I just couldn't get up the nerve. Then one day, I gotta letter from Ty that sounded like he wanted to give up and I couldn't let him do that," I explained.

"So you risked your life to go see my brother," she asked me her eyes getting wide.

"I had to, Nel," I said, my voice strained, "and when we sat across from one another, both of us speechless, it was electric. It was so intense, man," I said, thinking back on that day.

"Tammy, I had no idea," she said, a strange look coming over her face, "you're an angel."

I laid back, the meds making me drowsy.

"No, you're the angel, baby girl. I just wish you'd take better care with your heart and your body. Don't end up like me, loving the wrong man for half your life and then, when you find true love, he's practically married with twins on the way."

My eyes hung low and I felt myself becoming unconscious. Before I succumbed to sleep, the realization of my life and my wasted youth set it.

# Anthony

I sat in my kitchen at the table, my divorce papers staring back at me. My phone vibrated, it was Beth trying to get up with me again. She had become a nuisance in less than twenty four hours. I put my phone down and picked up the papers, reading them word for word. It couldn't really be over. She wanted the house, the kids, was willing to give me two thousand month in spousal support. Like she was paying me to step the fuck off.

I threw the papers back onto the table so hard that they scattered onto the floor. I snatched my phone up off the table and called my wife. She answered on the first ring sounding like she'd been crying.

"Hello?"

"Sam baby, I really want to talk about this. Can you meet me somewhere? Anywhere? So we can talk this out?" I begged.

I wasn't ready to lose her yet.

"Kris, I can't right now. I've got more important things to worry about."

"What's more important than our marriage? Our family? Our kids? Look, I know I haven't been the best to you, but I can change. I don't want to lose you," I was pleading harder than Keith Sweat.

"Look Kris, *not right now*," she said through sniffles and clenched teeth.

I looked down at the papers scattered across the table and the floor, the last page catching my eye. She hadn't signed the papers. I smiled when I saw the blank line on top of her name. She didn't want the divorce. She probably felt like she had no choice because she's pregnant but we can raise those children together just like we did my outside kids. And I could put that fuck nigga Tyrone in his place.

He and Sheila had caused nothing but problems since they come into our lives, but what could you expect from wards of the state and a crack whore's babies. Getting my dick wet wasn't worth losing my wife and that nigga sure as hell wasn't gonna be living it up while I got a measly fuckin' allowance. Samantha was mine, wasn't no two ways about it.

I realized that Sam hadn't hung up the phone. She was sitting there, sniffling, waiting for me to say something.

"I love you, baby," I said, "always have always will. No other woman could ever take your place. Let's just sit down and talk this out okay? Breakfast tomorrow morning?"

"I feel the same way, Kris. I mean, I love you and no other man has ever made me feel like you make me feel. But the cheating and the lies, the embarrassment of all the shit you do come to the light, I can't put myself or the children through that shit anymore," she confessed, frustrated.

"I can stop. I will stop. I mean it this time. The divorce papers hit home *hard.* You'd never even threatened divorce before. I get it, baby, just please come home and we can fix this. Counseling, whatever it takes, I'm willing to do it."

"It's too late for all that, Kris. I'm pregnant with another man's babies. Tyrone has been good to me and I don't want to fuck that up to come back to you and wind up dealing with the same bullshit," she said opening up a little.

"Okay, don't come home. Just please don't sign anything yet and please don't have another nigga around our kids. Let's not upset them until we get everything figured out, okay?"

"Fine Kris. I'll come to the house and eat breakfast with y'all tomorrow morning and we can talk after that," she finally conceded.

I smiled at my victory, as small as it was, and decided to get off the phone before she changed her mind. I decided not to tell her that the kids were with my sister for the night so it would be just me and Sam having breakfast.

"I love you, Samantha," I said, seductively into the phone.

"I love you, too, Kris," she replied, up the phone.

I smiled broadly, collecting the divorce papers and walking over to the fireplace. I threw them in there and watched as they burned when I threw match onto them. Even though it was summer, I let the flame eat away at the dissension that came between my wife and I. Tyrone Price ain't got shit on the history Sam and I have and that would be my ace in the hole. I went online and planned a family vacation. Sam was as good as home.

My phone vibrated again. I knew it was Beth. I knew that I shouldn't but now that I had Sam coming to breakfast in the morning I decided to answer her texts. Nothing like digging up in some tight, virgin pussy to celebrate my inevitable win.

# Sheila

I stared at Tammy laying in the hospital bed all bruised up and drugged up after giving years and years to Tre's no good ass and realized if it hadn't been for my brother that could've been me. I was so happy that motherfucker was locked up and would make sure that they put his ass under the jail. I was going to thank Tyrone for the sacrifices he made for me when he got here in the morning.

I was worried about him now though, with the babies on the way and Sam still being married to Anthony. I knew that Sam's heart was still in his grasp. I'd seen the way she looked at him when she and Ty were leaving the courthouse. That, paired with the fact that just like me and Tammy, she loved hard and had a propensity to give her heart to the wrong man, was a recipe for disaster.

I liked Sam well enough and knew she cared for my brother, but seeing him with Tammy tonight kinda made me wish she would go back to her husband and let Ty and Tammy have each other. I really wanted to see where my brother's head was at because I could tell when he left tonight his heart was torn. It was kind of ironic that a man who never had enough love growing up had more love than he knew what to do with now.

My heart ached for him. Looking at my brother's dilemma put things into perspective for me with Anthony. Tyrone was a good guy. He found himself in a sticky situation because he had such a big heart. Anthony, on the other hand, did what he did for an ego stroke. He loved having women waiting their turn for little of his time. The night that I got into it with Delilah, he was in heaven. The fact that he was inside the house when it happened but Tyrone was the one to get that bitch off of me proved it. I felt like he was sitting there watching it go down. I'd really wanted to believe Ant cared for me but nothing but his mouth said he did. And I had to pull that outta him. Then him fuckin' Delilah while I was at the doctor and even the way he looked at Tammy while I was laying up in the hospital bed, where indicators that Anthony didn't love anyone but Anthony. He was always in pursuit of his next nut, his next conquest.

"I'd rather be single and be someone's fool," I proclaimed aloud and Tammy shifted a little in her sleep.

I settled into trying sleep so that I didn't look like the walking dead at work tomorrow. With the abortion, a breakup, a cancer diagnosis, an ass whoopin', Tammy getting shot, and worrying about my brother, it would be a miracle if I could stand up straight. Tomorrow was definitely a flats kind of day. But I had a meeting with a hot new promoter who had been making waves in Birmingham, Miami, and Atlanta that I wanted on my payroll. I definitely wanted him for the grand opening of the Mojo Lounge.

Right before I dozed off, my phone vibrated. It was Tyrone checking on Tammy. I updated him and told him to go to bed. Laughing to myself, I put my phone down, got as comfortable as I could in the recliner, and drifted off to sleep.

*****

I woke up just as the sun peeked through the blinds. Tammy was still sound asleep and I could tell her body was grateful for the rest. I'm sure she was always on edge sleeping beside Tre. Just from what I saw him do to her with his belt, I could only imagine what else he was capable of. I sighed watching her rest, and got up to get ready for work. I took my overnight bag into the bathroom, washed my face and brushed my teeth before turning on the shower. I heard the nurse's cart rattle into the room and peeked my head out of the bathroom door to make sure they didn't need anything before I got completely undressed. When I got the green light from the nurse and a barely awake Tammy, I closed the door and pulled out my Bath and Body Works Brown Sugar and Pear body wash.

I hopped into the shower and lathered up. I started to get my mind set for my meeting. I'd chosen a power suit, gray with black pinstripes and a pencil skirt. I wanted to show him I meant business. I washed myself, rinsing off so I could apply my makeup and grab Tammy and I something to eat because I hadn't heard anything from Tyrone. I got out of the shower and dried off, lotioned up, and pulled out my clothes. I was putting on my foundation when I heard Ty come through the door.

"Special delivery!" He said loudly.

I pulled the door open and shushed him, thinking that Tammy was still sleep. But to my surprise, she was sitting up beaming at him. Laughing, I closed the door and went back to getting ready. I put on everything but my lipstick so that I didn't ruin it eating breakfast. I walked out of the bathroom and Tammy and Ty were rolling with laughter about something.

I sat my bag back in the chair and walked over to the bed.

"You get my order right?" I asked, poking Tyrone playfully.

"Nope," he said handing me my bag.

I walked back to the chair, moved my overnight bag to the floor, and sat down to eat.

"So, Miss Executive," Tammy teased, "you got any big meetings today?"

"Actually, yeah," I said with a mouth full of biscuit, "I'm meeting with a promoter for the grand opening of the Lounge. He's been making noise all over the Southeast and I want him on my team."

"That's what's up," Ty said, proudly, "You're doing big things, baby girl. I always knew you would."

I blushed as I stuffed my face. I was in a hurry. I wanted to take Jeff to school and get to the office in time to get my head together. I was so worried about this meeting. He just moved to the area and I knew he was a hot commodity but my rep had granted me first dibs. I just had to come with the follow-through. Shawn had been putting together the offer so I knew it was flawless, I just needed to familiarize myself with it.

I finished up my breakfast and threw the bag in the trash on my way to say my goodbyes. Tyrone was sitting on the side of the bed and hadn't moved since he'd gotten there. I kissed him on the cheek and gave him the "we need to talk" look to which he nodded his agreement. I touched Tammy tenderly on the hand.

"I'm headed out, love," I said, "but I'm sure this old man will take good care of you."

I laughed to myself at the unintended pun. The two of them blushed like they'd been caught in the act. I laughed and walked off smugly, grabbing my overnight bag on my way out the door. Turning around, I smiled again at two of the most important people in my life.

"You two *behave*," I said in my mama tone of voice. I laughed a little, "call me if you need anything," I said more seriously.

"Yes ma'am," they said sarcastically and in unison.

I left, laughing and my mind at ease because I knew that Tammy was safe from Tre and in good hands in more ways than one, with Ty. Driving to my foster mom's house, I called to let her know I was coming and to make sure Jeff was ready. She sounded a bit disturbed on the phone but I could tell it was something she didn't want to get into in front of Jeff. I felt my foot get heavy on the gas. I didn't play about that woman, so whatever it was took first priority.

I whipped into her driveway and got out of the car in a hurry. I walked into the house.

"Hey Mama," I yelled letting her know it was me walking in.

"Nel," my foster mom said, coming out of the kitchen, wiping her hands on her apron, "come here lemme look at you."

She gave me a tight hug and then held me at arm's length, taking me in. I did the same. She'd cut her salt and pepper hair really short. I could see her soft green eyes peeking from beneath her bangs. The skin around her eyes had crow's feet canyons carved into them and her laugh lines creased the corners of her then mouth as she smiled.

"You look great, Penelope," she said excitedly.

"So do you, Mama," I said smiling.

She let me go and rubbed her short cut in the back self-consciously.

"You like it? I know it's kind of drastic but who has time to do hair with everything else I've got going on," she explained herself.

"I love it, Mama! It flatters your face and lets those emeralds shine," I said kissing her on the cheek.

"You got a second?" She asked, her forehead creasing.

"I always have time for you," I said pulling the chair from the dining room table. She pulled out a chair as well.

"Jeff, hurry up child! Your mama and I gone talk for minute but then she gone be ready to go," she yelled down the hallway.

"Yes ma'am," Jeff yelled from the bathroom.

"What's up, Mama," I asked, worried, "you okay?"

"Yeah, I'm fine but..." She said, her voice trailing off.

"But what, you're scaring me," I said, my eyes getting wide.

"I had a visitor last night before I came to get Jeff from the hospital. How's Tammy doing by the way?" She asked, getting away from the subject.

"She's fine, Mama. Tyrone is up there with her," I was getting irritated.

"That's nice," she said, slowly like she was collecting her thoughts, "how is he?"

"He's great, got twins on the way. I'll tell you all about everything that's been going on with all of us if you just *please* get to the point," I begged.

She folded her hands in her lap then unfolded them. I had known Julianne Ferguson for most of my life and could count on one hand the number of times I'd seen her worry. I felt my blood began to boil. I knew it wasn't money because I paid all the bills here and she was damn near a saint so I knew she wasn't in any kind of trouble.

"Penelope... Nel... Sheila," she stammered. She almost never call me by my first name. "I need you to remain calm, okay?"

"Yes ma'am," I said willing to say anything to get her to spill the beans.

"I was getting ready to come to the hospital and there was a knock on the door. I opened it and there was a woman standing there. I thought she was a Jehovah's Witness but after taking another look at her with her bleached blonde hair, long fake nails, and to tight clothes, I knew she wasn't. When she spoke to me, she had an open-faced gold on one of her front teeth. She said that her name was Tanisha Price and she had gotten information that I was the woman who had adopted the daughter she was looking for."

My breath caught in my throat while I listened. I had never had any interest in meeting my birth mother. I sure as hell had no desire to now with all that I have going on.

"Did you tell her anything about me?" I asked nervously.

"No baby, of course not. I'd protect you with my last breath. I told her that I was a foster parent and that there had been many children that lived here and some of their names have been changed. But, Nel..." She said her eyes filling with tears.

"But what mama?" I asked reaching out to touch her hands. She was shaking.

"Your eyes, Nel. She had your eyes," she said tears running down her cheeks.

I sat silently, watching her wipe the tears from her flushed cheeks. She felt guilty lying to my real mother but she did what any mother would do to protect her child.

"You did the right thing, Mama," I reassured her. "I don't want to know her. She was probably looking for me to ask for money or something. Who waits twenty fuckin' years to find their children?"

"Watch your mouth, Penelope Price," she said instinctively.

"See," I laughed, "that's a real mama right there. I'm almost thirty with a child of my own and still can't cuss in your house."

She laughed with me wiping the tears from her eyes. Jeff came down the hallway backpack bouncing on his back. I got up and looked at my foster mom's smile-creased face.

"Hey there," I greeted my son with a hug. "You ready to go?"

"Yes ma'am," he said looking back and forth between me and my foster mom.

"Have a great day," she said rising from her seat and wrapping him up in one of her famous hugs.

"I'm going to call you after my meeting Mama, okay," I said, reaching out to grab her hand. "We've got a few things to discuss, maybe over dinner? I could definitely use some of your meatloaf in my life."

"Meatloaf it is," she said smiling, "we'll talk soon."

Jeff and I walked out to the car. I checked my watch for the first time since I'd gotten out of the car. That conversation had felt like it'd taken forever but I was still way ahead of schedule. I let out a sigh of relief but the information I'd been given weighed heavily on me. I pushed it out of my mind.

"So big head it, we need to talk, huh?" I asked, trying to lighten the mood.

"Mama, why did my daddy beat up Tammy like that?" he asked his mind heavy with thoughts.

"Your dad is angry, baby. Very angry. He doesn't know how to express his anger in a healthy way, so he used violence," I tried my best to explain.

"But he never hit me," he pointed out, "like never spanked me. Did he ever hit you?" he asked.

"Once," I admitted, "a long, long time ago. That's why your uncle went to prison. He beat your dad up for hitting me," I explained, choosing to leave out that he jumped on me because I wouldn't have an abortion. I never wanted my son to feel unwanted.

Jeff got quiet for a while. He seemed to be digesting everything I'd just told him. He looked at me, sniffling. At the red light, I looked back at him and saw him in tears. Something inside of me broke. It was my job to guard my child from the horrors of the world but how was I supposed to guard him from half of himself. *The sins of the father*, I thought to myself.

A horn blew behind me letting me know that the light had changed. I started driving but felt defeated, helpless.

"Mama, do you think I'll be like him?" he asked

I pulled the car to the side of the road. My eyes were leaking, I could barely see my son's face. I reached over and grabbed his face in my hands.

"You are nothing like your father," I said. "You may look like him but you are not a monster. You have the choice to stay the sweet, loving person you are, do you hear me?"

"Yes ma'am," he sniffled. "I'd never hurt a woman like that. Miss Tammy is nice and she did everything she could to make him happy. I just think of all those nights I heard them fighting and her crying and think he was probably hitting her and I could've stopped him," he confessed.

"There was nothing you could do to stop him, baby, and that's not your responsibility. Your dad is going to be punished for what he did to Tammy. Don't beat yourself up about him. He made his bed, you hear?"

"Yes ma'am," he said wiping his face. "I'm sorry you met my dad, and I'm sorry Miss Tammy met him, too."

"I'm not sorry," I said signaling to get back on the road. "I got you out of the deal, so I'd say I'm winning."

He smiled and we rode the rest of the way to Brew Tech in a peaceful silence. He had accepted my reasoning and that was all that mattered. I'd deal with my broken heart later. Jeff kissed me on the cheek before he got out of the car. It was an uncharacteristic act, especially in front of his classmates, but all things considered I just accepted it as a sign that my day was going to start looking up.

I got to the job in record time and jumped out of the car trying to regain every second I could, even though I was still an hour ahead of schedule.

"Good morning Miss Price. Ooh! Everything all right?" Shawn, my administrative assistant asked.

"Yeah, things are as good as can be expected given the circumstances," I said not sure why he felt the need to ask.

"O... K," he said, slowly "I've got coffee brewing and my final draft of the offer for your nine-thirty is on your desk," he said still staring.

"Shawn!" I snapped.

"Ma'am?" He asked nervously.

"What is it?" I asked wanting to know why he was staring at me like he was.

"Well, um," he stuttered, "you've got mascara streaks down your face like you been crying," he pointed out.

"Oh shit!"

I ran into my office and checked my reflection in the wall mirror. I looked a fool. I went into my purse and pulled out my makeup pouch. I fixed my makeup and walked over to my desk to go over Shawn's offer. My phone rang. It was Tyrone.

"Hey. Everything okay?" I asked.

"Yeah, everything's cool. They're releasing Tammy. I'm going to take her to her apartment to get some clothes and then she's agreed to let me take her to your house. Said y'all discussed it last night," he gave me the good news.

"Yeah, we did," I said smiling from ear-to-ear, "thanks for keeping me posted. You got your key? I'm going to my foster mom's for dinner but then I'll be headed straight to the house."

"Yeah, I do. I'll stay with her 'til you get home and may come back and help tonight, too," he offered.

I didn't respond. I'd get in my brothers ass later about leaving Sam at his apartment pregnant while he tended to Tammy. He needed to pick a damn side of the fence to be on. Both of these women were going through serious relationship transitions. Leading either of them on, intentionally or unintentionally, was not a good look.

"Our mother was at my foster mom's last night looking for me," I said changing the subject. "Mama lied to her and told her that she couldn't be sure if I'd lived with her," I summed up what I'd been told.

"Tanisha Price?" he asked, trying to make sure he'd heard me right.

"Yes, Ty. I'm not interested in meeting her or getting to know her. I think she wants money or something. She's twenty years past trying to reunite her family. Hell, we've got families of our own to worry about."

Tyrone held the phone. I would've thought the call had dropped if I hadn't heard him breathing.

"Miss Price," Shawn came over the intercom.

"Yeah Shawn," I said after telling Tyrone to hold on.

"There's someone here to see you," he said.

"My nine thirty is here early?" I asked both shocked and impressed. I hoped there was a miscommunication of some sort.

"No ma'am," Shawn said clearing his throat. His paused, alarming me.

"Come into my office, please Shawn," I said.

The intercom hung up. Seconds later, he walked in closing the door behind him quickly.

"What's up, Shawn?" I asked. "You're actin' like the cops are out there waitin' for me or somethin'," I tried to make a joke.

"Sheila," he said, dropping the formalities, "there's a woman at the Receptionist's Desk who says she's your mother. I went up there because they paged down here for an escort to your office. When I got up there, I saw why. She's got…"

"Platinum blonde hair, an open-faced gold tooth in the front of her mouth, too small clothes, and long ass fake fingernails," I finished his statement for him.

"Yeah," he said, his face twisting up.

"She was at my foster mom's house last night, lookin' for me, that's why I know," I explained.

"So, what do you want me to do?" he asked. "She's in the lobby."

I sighed. I wanted to tell him to blow her off but I had a feeling she wouldn't stop coming up here and I didn't need that kind of shit at my place of business. I thought about sending Shawn back up to the lobby with a check and a note informing her that I would call the police if she didn't leave me alone. I was at a loss and didn't have time for this shit. I was supposed to be preparing for my meeting.

My office phone rang reminding me to Tyrone was still on hold.

"She's here, Ty," I said once I picked up the phone.

"Who's there?" Tyrone asked, concerned.

"Shawn, can you give me just a second and I'll let you know how we're going to handle the situation," I asked covering the mouthpiece of the phone.

He nodded and walked out of the office, a look of concern and frustration on his face.

"Tanisha Price done brought her ass to my job," I said.

"Damn, Nel," he sighed, "want me to come up there?"

"Now, I'm thinking about writing her a check and telling her I'll call the cops if she ever tries to contact me again," I said. "How much do you think is a good fuck off amount?"

Tyrone couldn't help laughing even though he knew I was dead ass serious.

"She's our mother, Nel," he tried to rationalize, "as fucked up a job as she may have done at it, we at least owe it to her to see what made her come looking for you after all these years. I'm curious to know why myself because she hasn't come looking for me."

I heard a hint of pain in his tone. I knew it hurt him that she'd made no efforts to find him.

"Ty, don't spend another moment feeling bad because she ain't knocking down doors looking for you. She ain't worth the grief, but," I paused thoughtfully, knowing what needed to be done, "I think I've got away to get some answers for both of us. Can you meet me here around noon for lunch?"

"Yeah, sure," Tyrone said reluctantly not knowing what I had planned.

"Great, see you then," I said and hung up.

"Shawn," I said, my finger on the intercom button, "tell Reception I'll be right there."

I checked my makeup again before walking out of my office. I touched Shawn on his shoulder when I passed him, pausing for a moment to let him see that I was okay.

"Can you..."

"Prepare everything for your nine thirty. Already done," he said.

"Thank you," I smiled. "And I'm gonna need you to brief me on your offer because I haven't had a second to sit still and for damn days," I admitted, frustrated that I'd allowed myself to get so distracted.

"I got you," Shawn said with a wink.

I straightened my blazer and walked towards the lobby. My heart fell to my feet when I saw the woman sitting there waiting for me. Her face was hard like she'd seen too many demons in her lifetime. She tried to cover it up with too much makeup. Her hair was cut into a short Afro that was bleached blonde and she had on a two small green tank top with her breasts stuffed into it and a pair of black leggings. She had on a pair of black wedge heels with a French pedicure on her toes. Her fingernails were long and curled from her fingers. There were rhinestone studs glued to them.

She stood up, a smile coming across her full lips revealing her teeth, the open-faced gold tooth peeking through.

"Sheila Penelope Price, would you look at you," she said loudly, poking out her chest.

"Hello, Mrs. Price," I said formally, keeping my distance.

"Don't be like that, child. I gave birth to you," she said balling her face up.

"And that's about all that you've done for me," I said unable to hide my anger. "You know what? Now's not the time or the place for this. I'm at *work*. I don't know why you're here or what you want for me but I plan to find out. Can you come back here at noon and we'll go to lunch?"

"Sure," she was taken back by my professional tone.

"See you then," I said, turning on my heels and walking back towards my office.

I checked my watch, shaking my head the amount of time I'd wasted on emotional baggage. I was sure that this wasn't good for my health. Stress fuels cancer and I was stressed to the fuckin' max right now. I walked into my office with Shawn on my heels.

"Now let's get some business handled, shall we?" I asked sitting in my plush leather office chair and opening the folder sitting on my desk.

"Absolutely," Shawn agreed leaning forward to catch me up before my meeting.

# Samantha

"Tyrone, you left here before the damn sun was all the way up. What in the hell was so important? I made yo' ass breakfast," I yelled into the phone.

"I had to come to the hospital to sit with Tammy, baby," he explained, his tone hushed like him talking to me was supposed to be a secret.

"Why is she your responsibility?" I asked.

"She's like family, Sam," he explained, "She got shot and doesn't have anybody else. She's done so much for my family that this the least I can do."

"And why did she get shot, Ty? Because she was living with the fuckin' drug dealer who's been beating her ass?" I asked annoyed.

"You're talking like you know something about her and her life," he said, his voice getting thick and full of base.

"I don't know nothing but what you told me. But, judging by the blood on the clothes in the fuckin' laundry basket, your felon ass was there when she got shot! What the fuck is the matter with you? You act like you ain't just get out of jail. Being tied up with Tammy and Tre had your ass locked up for twelve goddamned years, and now you back over there in the middle of they shit," I replied, getting heated.

"Tammy ain't have shit to do with me going to prison," he defended her like I knew he would. "She was one of the only reasons I didn't lose my mind when I *was* locked up. But see, you don't know nothing about that 'cause you were living in marital bliss with a nigga who had baby number thirty on the way with another woman," he said, his voice raised now.

I sucked in air. What he'd just said to me stung, but not as much as the fact that he was really choosing Tammy over me.

"Tyrone!" I yelled tears running down my cheeks.

"Sam, look," he said, regretting his tone. "Can we talk about this when I get home? I've had an emotional enough day. I'm sorry for taking it out on you."

"I may not be here when you get here. You obviously need time to get your feelings and your priorities in order."

"Come on, Sam, don't be that way. We can talk about this when I get home, please—"

I hung up the phone and sat on the bed. I looked across the room at the bloody clothes on the floor. I'd almost had a heart attack when I saw them earlier. Sheila had told me that Tammy had gotten shot and I put two and two together. Then,

Tyrone had the nerve to leave at the fuckin' crack of dawn, not telling me where he was going and hadn't come back for breakfast yet. My suspicions were confirmed when I called to find out that he's at the hospital by Tammy's side. He was there tending to her when he should have been at home with me. I didn't want to feel this way, but I felt like I did so many nights waiting for Kris to come home. Rejected. Inadequate. Ready to tear some shit up.

Becoming infuriated, I went into the bathroom and washed my face. I looked at my reflection and then decided that this would be the last time I shed tears over a man. I went into the kitchen and scraped the grits, eggs, waffles, and turkey sausage into the trash can. Stomping back to the bedroom, I snatched my suitcase out the closet and pulled the drawers open.

I started throwing my clothes into the empty luggage. I went back into the bathroom and collected all of my things from toothbrush to curling iron to body wash. I took them and stuffed them into my suitcase, sitting on top of it to close it.

My phone rang and Kris's face popped up on the screen. I smiled but became filled with of hesitation. Before I saw his face, I was hell-bent on going back home to him. But now, sitting there looking at the heartless monster that I'd left behind, I began to second-guess my rash decision. I had no proof that Tyrone was cheating on me. It was quite possible that he was just being there for family friend, one who had been there for both him and his sister. My husband though...he had taken me through a decade of hell and embarrassed me for the entire world to see.

I answered the phone on the last ring before the voicemail caught it.

"Hey Kris," I said, not really sure what I had to say to him.

"You stood me up for breakfast," he said sounding sad.

"I'm sorry, something came up."

"I bet it did," he said sarcastically.

I sighed heavily into the phone. His nastiness just didn't stop. It never did.

"Kris, I'll be there in a little while," I said, conceding.

"I'm not home. I just called to tell you that I met with an attorney and he shared some interesting insights on this divorce nonsense. So, if you're headed to the house, we can talk about it when you get there, Sam."

"Okay," I said, feeling the hair standing up on the back of my neck. Knowing Kris, he could be headed in any direction over my wanting a divorce.

I hung up and lugged the suitcase off the bed. I was grateful that it was a roller. Carrying it would've been too much. I stopped in the living room and picked up my purse from the couch and my keys from the end table. I looked around at what I was leaving behind. The many memories that had been made within these walls flooded my mind. Even after all that we'd overcome to be together, Tyrone was still too entangled with Tammy for us to ever have anything meaningful. I blinked away the memories we'd shared in this place as quickly as they came and walked out the door, making sure to lock the door behind me. I made my way down the stairs and packed the car with my measly belongings. I was on my way back home.

# Tyrone

I walked back into the hospital and got on the elevator, wiping my face with both hands. I didn't want to worry Tammy when I got back to her room. I patted my thigh with my thumb and forefinger in a steady rhythm trying to calm myself. I walked slowly to Tammy's room, taking deep breaths and counting backwards from twenty. I forced a smile on my face when I reached her door.

She was standing up collecting her things as best she could with one good arm. They'd put the other one in a brace and asked her to limit use of it outside of her physical therapy.

"Woman, what do you think you're doing?" I asked laughing to myself.

"Well, you were gone and I'm ready to get the fuck up out of here. I just got my walking papers," she said trying to pull her shirt over her head.

"Tammy," I said rushing to help her.

This woman was stubborn as hell but I thought that was endearing. I helped her put on her pants and shoes before picking up her purse and the bag Nel have packed her before she tried to carry them herself.

"Don't we have to wait for someone to come with the wheelchair to escort us downstairs?" I asked.

"Nigga, you watch way too much television," Tammy said laughing. "All I gotta do is pay my bill, or my deductible at least, and we can go."

I laughed and we walked towards the cashier's window. I went to get the car while she spoke to the cashier. I didn't want to be standing there when Tammy found out her bill had been paid in full. It was the least I could do. I pulled up to the front door and waited. She got in the car with a huge grin on her face.

"Which of y'all did it?" she asked putting on her seatbelt.

"Did what?" I asked playing dumb.

"Really, Tyrone," she said, giving me the side eye as we pulled off.

"Yes, really," I refused to reveal who had paid her hospital bill.

She huffed and turned up the radio, looking out of the window. We neared her apartment complex and I felt her body tense up. I took one hand off of the steering wheel and grabbed her hand. I parked but neither of us moved to get out of the car. The car was still and silent and it hurt me to feel the fear radiating off of her when we both knew Tre was in jail.

"He's gone," I told her wanting to calm her. "You'll be fine. I'm here with you and you know I'm not gonna let anything happen to you."

"Ty," Tammy said squeezing my hand and looking past me, "that's Scooter's car over there. He's either here to kill me or he's looking for the cash stash."

"Which one?" I asked so I could commit it to memory.

"The gold Honda right there two spaces down," she motioned with her head.

"Aight, let's go." I put the car reverse and pulled out of the parking lot. "You really think he'd be here to kill you? How would he even know when you were discharged?"

"His baby mama is a nurse. She probably checked my records and saw the discharge papers," she explained.

"But that will make her an accessory if he kills you. She can't be that fuckin' stupid."

Tammy gave me a look that sent a chill down my spine.

"How stupid does she have to be, Tyrone? How stupid was I to stay with Tre all these years? Through the ass whoopings and the cheating. Do you know how many bitches have jumped on me over Tre only for me to get home and have him jump on me, too? These niggas brainwash you and trust, she wants that money and Tre out of jail so him and Scooter can keep dealing. I'm the only thing in the way of that now."

Tammy's voice was shaking but I knew she was dead serious. I drove past Nel's house and onto my apartment complex. I didn't want Scooter coming looking for Tammy at my sister's house. I'd just have to explain it to Sam and she could either get with it or go back to her husband. I had a feeling she had one foot out the door headed back to the nigga anyway.

I parked in front of my building and didn't see Sam's car. I helped Tammy out the car and up the stairs. I opened the door to find my house and shambles. The sink was filled with dishes and pots that I knew had held the food that had been thrown in the trash. The bathroom was absent of any of Sam's stuff and the drawers were pulled open and emptied where her clothes had once been.

*This woman has a serious flight complex,* I thought to myself, *at the first sign of conflict she's out the door.*

I wasn't going to be an option for her anymore. Being her escape was nice at first but she's pregnant with my children now and I was seriously considering proposing to her at the grand opening whether she was married or not. But she was starting to show me why a man would get frustrated with her. She made a man feel like he wasn't needed, on a completely different level. Having money and options was one thing, but knowing that your woman could just up and get ghost made a man feel useless.

I wanted to call her but had more taxing issues at hand. I had to get Tammy settled and go to Nel's job because my mother had decided to resurface and hunt my sister down. I wanted to leave here and have enough time to go back and see if Scooter was still at her house. The women in my life had me exhausted, but it was my job as their protector to make sure that they were okay.

"What tornado tore through here?" Tammy asked sitting on the bed and looking around the room.

"Tropical Storm Samantha," I said laughing and shaking my head.

"Oh hun, it's not because of me, is it?" she asked.

"No. Well, not really," I answered honestly. "She has mixed feelings about being with me and being with her husband."

"That sucks. Especially because she's having your baby," she said thoughtfully.

"*Babies*," I corrected her, "she's having twins. But yeah, this is a pretty fucked up situation. Anthony isn't gonna make it easy on me if he and Sam reconcile."

"She won't let that happen, though, right?"

"I can't say, Tam," I admitted sitting down beside her on the bed. "I've been dealing with Sam as a married woman. I was her side piece, ya know. But being with her more often and getting to know her as someone I want to be with for the rest of my life, I'm finding some things I really don't like."

"Well that's to be expected, love," she rationalized, "you learn a person's quirks when you're in their space like that. I'm sure there will be things about me that would drive you crazy if we were in each other's space all the time."

"I doubt it," I said scooting closer to her.

"Believe it," she looked up at me with tears dripping into her lap.

"Well, I guess I'm about to find out, huh?" I wiped her tears away.

She gave me a weak smile and grabbed my hand with her good hand. She looked at me in a way that made my dick jump. I wanted her but I knew she was hurting and didn't want to take advantage of her. She was worth the wait to me and I had shit to attend to, Samantha included. I didn't pass up the opportunity to kiss her, though. I kissed her long and hard like I used to when we'd sneak away. Years of wanting her all to myself and now I had her and I didn't want to do anything but be with her, hear her laugh, feel her body pressed against mine.

My phone rang making me break loose of Tammy. I reached into my pants pocket and answered it. The pharmacy was calling to let me know that Tammy's meds were ready. I hung up and looked at Tammy. She was so vulnerable that I hated to leave her.

"I'll be back as soon as I can, okay?" I assured her. "The remote is in the nightstand, there's plenty to eat and drink in the fridge."

"I'll be fine, Ty. I'm going to get some sleep."

I kissed her again then headed for the door. I was headed back to her house and then on to Nel's job to find out what the fuck Tanisha Price wanted with her.

Hopefully by then Sam and I would be able to talk calmly and come to an understanding about what we wanted to do... About everything.

# Anthony

I pulled into my garage and found Sam's car parked in its spot. I smirked at the fact that she'd beat me here. Collecting the papers from my meeting with my attorney. I opened the door, ready to force her back against the wall and make her bring her ass home, hopefully for good this time. The thought of Tyrone's kids calling me daddy made me smile even bigger.

I walked into the house to find Sam sitting at our table crying, a pair of panties in her hand.

*Oh shit, Beth,* I thought, wishing I hadn't let her ass come over here. I should've gone to her house but was being lazy and the bitch had left her underwear at my house, obviously marking territory.

"It's never going to stop, is it?" Samantha asked, her face wet but her eyes burning into me.

My mind raced trying to come up with a lie that would keep her here long enough for me to seal the deal and end this divorce mess. I couldn't think of anything that would make sense.

"Sam look," I said choosing to be honest with her. "I was lonely, okay. I mean how do you think I feel knowing that my wife was playing house with another nigga and is pregnant with his babies?"

"So now it's my fault you can't keep your fuckin' dick to yourself? How about all the other times, huh? Before the pregnancy? Before Tyrone? How many STDs have I been treated for because you don't have enough respect for me to put on a damn rubber? And Sheila was just pregnant, wasn't she?"

She was right. I'd put her through hell and she'd hung on, even when I was trying to shake her loose. I looked at the floor. I had nothing to say.

"Cat got your tongue?" she asked. I swear I could see steam rising from her head.

"No," I said, "you're right. About everything. I can't justify it. I'm just hoping we can get past it."

I reached for her hands but she pulled both of them back. She cried, loudly. I'd never seen her lose control like this. I mean, I was sure she cried when I didn't come home and I'd seen her shed tears when she found out about my other kids, but this cry was different. She cried like she'd broken. I really did love my wife and with all of the dirt I'd done, all the dirt I was still doing, I hated actually witnessing the damage

I'd done to her. Sam was the kind to get upset, get over it, and keep it moving. I didn't think she would this time.

"Who is she?" She asked.

I debated lying to her but changed my mind.

"Beth, the white waitress from the Egg & I," I confessed.

"Call her," she said more as an order than a request.

"Baby, you don't have to argue with her or anybody for that matter. This is between me and you," I begged.

"I have no intention on arguing with her. I'm going to resolve this once and for all," she said. "Call her or I'll pay her a visit at her job."

"Fine," I said scrolling through my contacts until I reached her number. Beth picked up on the second ring.

"Hey daddy," Beth greeted me seductively.

"Hey. Look, Sam wants to talk to you," I warned.

"Okay," she said calmly shocking and scaring me at the same time.

I handed the phone over to my wife, nervous for the first time in a long time.

"Hello Beth," Sam said, her voice showing no evidence of her tears. I sat back and listened not wanting to miss a single word.

"Yeah, I found what you left for me in the bedroom," Samantha said. "Mmm hmm... I'd really like for you to come over here so that we can do just that... Okay, see you in twenty, you remember how to get here, right... Great, bye."

Sam hung up the phone and gave it back to me. I got nervous because I had no idea what was coming next but I had made his bed, so I was gonna lay in it. I only hoped they hadn't just agreed to murder me. As ridiculous as that sounded I never put anything past a woman scorned. Hell, Sheila had committed murder when she aborted our baby. What was to keep Sam and Beth from doing the same?

*****

Twenty minutes or so later, I felt like I was having déjà vu. The only difference was that it was Beth sitting at the kitchen table instead of Delilah. And this was no job interview. I sat, nervously, waiting to see what would happen next.

"Beth, I invited you here because my husband, facing divorce, still fucked you. And in my house, no less," Sam said.

Her tone showed that she meant business and her body language, hands folded in front of her on the table, said the same thing.

"Mmm hmm," Beth said listening attentively.

"And you wanted to let me know that you'd been here, so you weren't going down without a fight," she kept going.

"He's the first man I've ever been with and he fucked the shit out of me. Well, I'm sure you know, you married him," Beth said.

I watched them both. They were both so calm. I wrung my hands because they were beginning to sweat.

"Well, I can say that's one thing he's definitely good at," Sam said laughing

Beth laughed in agreement. That lightened the mood a little.

"So how do we fix this?" Beth asked smiling across the table at Sam.

"How about this, I've never been with a woman and since my husband was your first man, I was hoping you'd return the favor. I'm tired of fighting women for time with Kris, so let's make it easy for him," she said smiling back at Beth.

I felt my eyes bulge. I couldn't believe what I was hearing. Was my wife not only willing to allow me to fuck another woman but be present and participate? It was too good to be true.

"Kris," Sam said snapping me out of my thoughts, "I love you. I'm tired of this foolishness so I'll agree to let you fuck Beth and only Beth. My only condition is that we fuck her together."

I smiled from ear-to-ear. I didn't know how this shit was going to go or how long it was going to last. Fuck, they could've still been planning to kill me. But I'll be damned if this wasn't a hell of a way to go.

"Are you for real right now?" I asked my wife looking from her to Beth and realizing they weren't playing.

"I'm as serious as a fuckin' heart attack," Sam said, "are you willing to keep your end of it?"

"Yeah," I said reluctantly, nodding.

She and Beth both got up from the table and walked into the Master Bedroom. I watched as they started kissing, the scene alone made my dick bone hard. I didn't get up right away. I enjoyed the show from my seat at the table. They were so involved in fuckin' each other that they hadn't looked at me once. I started to lose my erection when I realized that Sam had found a way to take the fun out of fuckin' another woman. I watched Beth undress her, sucking on her pregnancy-swollen nipples and diving in, eating her pussy like a life depended on it.

I watched my wife shake and hold Beth's head in place while she gyrated her hips, fuckin' her face. I found myself getting angry. I got up and walked into the bedroom, taking off my shirt and pants. Sam slid back onto the bed and Beth got up on the bed not slowing down her slurping. She was on all fours. Her dress slid up to reveal that she'd come to my house with no underwear on. I shoved my dick into her more forcefully than I had before, hoping to throw her off from pleasuring my wife who was now howling her name in pleasure. Beth took the dick and moaned her pain out on Sam's clit. I fucked Beth hard my hands on her shoulders holding her steady as I rammed her. Slapped her ass until it turned red, watching a jiggle with every thrust.

She tongue-fucked Sam in unison to my motions. I watched Sam's face contort and felt Beth tighten and cum on my dick. Sam shook in orgasm, too. I pulled out of Beth twice as frustrated as before. I stood there, dick barely hard, and looked at both of them. Sam gave me a smirk that let me know she knew exactly what she was doing.

I laid down on the opposite end of the bed trying to calm myself. This was every man's dream come true and I couldn't enjoy it because of my damned ego. I felt a mouth on my dick. Beth was completely oblivious to what was going on. She just wanted to fuck. I grabbed her head and pushed my dick into her mouth until she choked and her eyes watered.

"Ride this dick," I told her when I let her head go.

She climbed on top of me obediently.

"And you," I said looking at Sam, "come sit on my face," I ordered.

Sam straddled my face, facing Beth. They kissed each other, moaning into one another's mouths as I ate Sam's pussy until she locked up and Beth rode my dick until I squirted inside of her. I didn't let either move. I held both by their asses, making Sam cum again and shoving my new erection up into Beth. I would not be outdone. When I finished my dick was sore, but I had fucked and eaten Beth and Samantha until neither of them could take anymore.

I lay there, two women naked in my arms. Two women who were willing to share me just to have me. I felt sick to my stomach. I got even sicker when they began caressing one another, ready to start up again and I was down for the count. I closed my eyes and they went in on one another again, Beth climbing over me to get to Samantha.

My wife had won again. And my dumb ass had agreed to her terms. Fuck my life.

# Tammy

I laid in Tyrone's bed trying to rest but I couldn't sleep. Seeing Scooter's car outside of my apartment let me know that I wasn't free of Tre. I just knew that he'd sent him there. What they didn't know was that I had already sent Sheila back to the house to get the cash. I knew he'd come looking for it and wanted them to think that the cops had found and confiscated all of the money when they'd taken the drugs as evidence. I knew Scooter was going to wait until the heat had died down to go search the house.

More than the money worried me, though. I hadn't lied to Tyrone when I said Scooter probably intended to kill me. He and Tre would do anything for each other, but the reality was that Tre was the brains and Scooter was the muscle of the operation. Without Tre, well in reality, me telling Tre what moves to make, it would only be a matter of time before their shit fell apart and another nigga took their clientele.

I was sure that bitch had called Scooter and told him I'd been let go. And I was sure Scooter came to the house to kill two birds with one stone. I sat up and turned on the TV. I flipped through the channels and stopped on The View to see what foolery Raven Simoné was going to be up to today. That poor woman didn't believe in thinking before she spoke.

I saw their mouths moving but no words were breaking through as my thoughts ran rampant. My shoulder got tight and I reached over and got my Vicodin from the nightstand where Tyrone had left it for me next to a bottle of water he'd already broken the seal on for me. I pop the pill and sat back in Tyrone's bed and entertained the idea of actually being with him. I'd fantasized about it for so long but never thought it would be a reality.

*It's still not a reality,* I reminded myself, *as far as I know he's still with Sam and they've got babies on the way.*

That reality settled into me and I dismissed any thought to pursuing Tyrone as not to make a fool of myself. I got a funny feeling in my gut. Something that told me I needed to call Tyrone. Without a second thought, I picked up my cell phone and dialed his number. It went straight to voicemail. My heart started to race. I called Sheila but her phone went straight to voicemail, too. I knew she had a big meeting today so I knew she'd call me back.

I called the pharmacy to see if my meds had been picked up yet. They hadn't. I called Ty's cell phone again and panicked when it went to voicemail. I sent him a text asking him to call me ASAP then I sat waiting on a call back. I rocked nervously. The Vicodin kicked in and made me drowsy. I fought it for as long as I could before giving in and sliding beneath the covers. Before I went to sleep, I turned the volume all the way up so I heard Ty and Nel when they got around to calling back.

*****

I woke up not knowing how long I'd been asleep. I checked my phone and saw no missed calls from Tyrone or Nel. The clock read one thirty so I'd been asleep for a few hours. That Vicodin must've been magic because I felt refreshed and my arm wasn't hurting even a little bit. I decided to get up and take a shower. I took off my brace, laughing because I knew Tyrone would be furious if he knew what I was doing. I got undressed carefully, making sure not to overextend my shoulder. I'd wait until he got back to clean and redress my wound. I was grateful for the waterproof tape that it been placed on top of the hole in my shoulder and the nurse who'd shown me how to shower before I left the hospital because I would've gone insane if I'd had to take birdbaths for the next few weeks.

I went into the bathroom, turned on the shower, and sat on the toilet waiting for the water to get hot. I pulled a face towel from the linen stand and stepped into the steaming hot water. It felt good to be in a space alone cleaning myself. I didn't feel the need to leave the curtain cracked open or check for shadows like I had at home. I was finally accepting the fact that Tre was locked up and, even better, that Tyrone would never harm me like that.

I took my time cleaning every corner and crevice of myself. I wanted to be ready in case Tyrone decided he wanted to take things there. I knew he wouldn't, not with me on the rebound and him still in limbo with his situation with Samantha. I had to convince myself to be patient, maybe even sleep in his spare room as not to present any kind of temptation. Then as soon as the coast was clear, I was gonna haul ass to Nel's to stay with her and my baby boy Jeffrey so that Sam didn't resent me if things went badly between her and Tyrone.

I rinsed off and got out of the shower, wrapping myself in a towel. I had to say Tyrone was doing pretty well for himself. But I had to be honest with myself because I knew that a lot of things had a woman's touch. I wanted to think it was Nel but I knew it was probably Sam. He told me he'd been stacking his cash and Sam was caking him, but she was spending a grip on this apartment. I knew he wouldn't be willing to let go of all of that to be with a broke ass line worker like me, even with the money I'd gotten from the house.

I walked out of the bathroom going into the bedroom to check my phone and damn near jumped out of my skin.

"Sam, you scared the shit out of me," I said grabbing my heart with my right hand, the towel falling to the floor. My left arm wasn't strong enough to hold it up.

"Mmph, I see what's got Tyrone going," she said looking at me in a way that made me very uncomfortable.

I covered myself with my hands as best I could.

"I didn't know anyone was here," I said not sure why this woman had me shook.

I just wasn't in the mood for no drama. I walked over to the bed and picked up my shirt, struggling to put it on. I had it over my head but just couldn't lift my left arm to get it in the hole. Sam walked across the room. She got close enough for our bodies to touch. My skin began to crawl. She helped me into my shirt.

"You're real comfortable in my man's house," she said, her mouth on my ear.

"Thank you," I said being polite and thanking her for the help with my shirt.

I took a step back and looked Sam in the face. I turned my back to her to get my jeans, letting her know I didn't see her as a threat even though I did. I pulled on my pants before I looked at her again, or spoke.

"Sam I don't mean no disrespect. I was supposed to be going to Nel's... Sheila's house but Ty didn't think it was safe so he brought me here," I explained.

My phone started ringing on the bed. Usher and Alicia Key's song "My Boo" filling the room. I blushed and walked over to answer the phone.

"Tyrone, are you okay?" I asked. He'd scared the hell out of me.

"Yeah, I'm good," he lied. "I picked up your medicine, I'll be home in a little while. We got a lot to talk about."

"I hope it's good," I said trying not to smile too hard.

"Some of it, yeah," he said with a smirk in his voice.

"You can tell me about it on the way to Nel's house," I said letting him know that I was ready to go.

"Why the rush?" he asked sounding hurt that I wanted to leave. Then he got quiet and so did I. "I'll be there ASAP."

He hung up the phone and I put the phone down on the bed. "Tyrone's on his way," I told Sam.

I went to the living room to avoid threatening Sam's position as the woman of the house. I sat on the couch waiting for Tyrone to get to the house.

Samantha followed me up there and sat in the arm chair directly across from me. She crossed her legs in a smug sort of way.

"You like the apartment?" she asked, her eyes trained on me. "I picked it. Tyrone was sleeping on his sister's couch when I met him. A felon who'd just got a decent job. He was terrible with money. I taught him how to budget, bought him that car he brought you here in. I picked out that couch you're sitting on and the bed you were laying in."

"It's nice. You've got great taste."

"In everything but men it looks like," she said snickering like she'd said something funny.

"Sam don't do that. We've all had our bad relationships. What a man chooses to do has nothing to do with you or the woman you are," I tried to cheer her up.

"That would be believable if it wasn't coming from a chick who wasted her youth on a hustlin' ass nigga who was getting women pregnant left and right. Then spent more years than I've known Kris waiting on another one to get out of jail just for him to upgrade to a bitch like me while you were getting your ass kicked," she said looking at me with razorblade eyes.

I was a threat to her and she tried to hide it behind insults. I'd heard worse from Tre. Hell, I'd heard worse from Delilah when she needed to shit on somebody. I smiled and let her vent.

"See, I make men better. You have that ride or die syndrome. You wallow in the field with your man and call it loyalty. I put them in a mansion and train their asses. I make myself irreplaceable. You're just available," she said sounding insane.

"Yet your man, your *husband*, has been fuckin' around on you for as long as y'all have been together," I said calmly. "A nigga can only be what he is. No amount of money or *training* is going to change that. You're smart enough to know that, hun."

Sam sucked her teeth and looked like she wanted to slit my throat. But she didn't move. She talked big shit but she knew even with one arm that I would paint the walls with her motherfuckin' ass. I was glad she knew.

I remembered Sam from growing up with Delilah. Her mama was Dee's daddy's mistress. When he got locked up, she lost her mind waiting for him. They said she died of a broken heart. Rumor had it she'd saved all the hush money he paid her from the moment he found out she was pregnant and left it to Sam when she died along with the house and car he'd bought her. They said she was a millionaire when she died. That's why Sam threw money around like it was nothing. But she was continuing her mother's cycle. I guess the apple really doesn't fall too far from the tree.

I never broke eye contact with her, but her rubbing her stomach while she stared me down let me know that she *did* remember me. And she knew I couldn't have kids so she was sitting there rubbing the one thing I couldn't give Tyrone in my face. I felt my face begin to twitch.

*Why don't this bitch take her ass home to her trifling ass husband?* I thought to myself feeling my face get hot.

I wanted this bitch. And bad. But I was just gonna let Tyrone cut her ass loose and get mine being step-momma to her children.

I smirked at the thought. But I was saddened by the fact that I'd never be able to give Tyrone a child. That shit made me feel like a failure as a woman every time I thought about it. Tre took that for me with his venturing dick. Sam better be careful before Anthony did the same thing to her, or worse gave her something she couldn't get rid of. She was gonna end up like her mama, crazy as hell waiting for man to love her.

I heard keys in the door but kept my eyes locked with Sam's. Tyrone walked and she jumped up finally breaking eye contact with me. She wrapped her arms around Ty's neck and kissed him. She was marking territory. Tyrone's eyes drifted to me. He was confused as hell but wasn't trying to embarrass Sam, so he played along. He knew I was cool because it wasn't like him having a woman was a surprise to me. He knew I was gonna play my role.

"Hey baby," he greeted her when she finally let him go.

"How are you? Everything okay? Where have you been?" she faked concern, laying all over him.

She didn't know I knew about their argument and I wasn't going to be the one to tell her.

"I went to lunch with Nel and ran a few errands. Here's your medicine, Tammy," he said holding up the pharmacy bag.

Sam had her back to me but I could feel her rolling her eyes.

"Thank you," I said getting up and walking over to get my medicine, "I'll go get my things."

Tyrone sighed when I walked away towards the bedroom. I knew Sam wasn't gonna let me chill if I stayed over here. And I just wanted to chill. I'd get some peace at Nel's house and I wouldn't be rockin' no boats over there. I packed my things as fast as my one arm would let me.

Tyrone came into the room and started to help.

"What the hell did I walk into," he asked.

"Sam pissin' on a tree," I said laughing.

"I'm sorry about that, Bay," he said walking up behind me.

"Ty," I leaned my head back into his chest.

"Hmmm," he asked taking a deep whiff of my hair.

"Where's Sam?" I asked.

"In the bathroom taking a shower."

"I don't think it's a good idea for you to be disrespectin' Samantha like this," I said stepping away from him.

"Fuck her," he walked up to me and pulled me close to him.

"That's exactly why you're in the predicament you're in now," I said rolling my eyes. "That woman pays the bills in this house. What the hell do I look like fuckin' with you like this with her in the next room?"

"Good question," Sam said from the doorway, wrapped in a towel.

I stepped away from Tyrone and kept packing my things. I made sure to keep her ass in my peripheral view just in case she decided to try some dumb shit.

She stood there staring at Tyrone like she was awaiting an explanation. He looked at her then back at me before grabbing my duffel bag and walking towards the door. Sam didn't budge. Her body language challenged Ty and I felt the hair standing up on the back of my neck.

"Excuse me," Tyrone said with enough bass in his voice to rattle the windows.

Sam leered at him sucking her teeth. I felt myself holding my breath because I knew this could go one of two ways. I'd hate to have to whoop Sam's ass with my good arm. If she laid one finger on Tyrone, though, her as was as good as beat, pregnant or not.

"You better be glad I don't wanna show my ass in front of company, Tyrone. We'll talk after you drop your "friend" off," Samantha said stepping out of the way.

Tyrone walked past her and I picked up my purse and followed.

"Don't bring your ass back over here," Sam said to me under her breath when I walked by.

I didn't even respond, just looked her in the face, flashed a smile, and twitched my ass down the hallway to the door. Secondary bitches don't intimidate me. I walked down the stairs and got into the car with Tyrone.

# Sheila

Shawn showed his *ass* with that agreement for the promoter. I had a few minutes before my meeting so I went outside to smoke. I lit my clove trying to get my nerves together. This was a big deal for me, and Shawn, because he was going to get a percentage of any commission received from collaborations with this promoter. I was excited and had butterflies. I needed this meeting to go well but after the past three days I wouldn't be surprised if this was an epic fail. Then I was meeting my birth mom and Tyrone for lunch, which I wasn't looking forward to. I smoked my Djarum to the filter, flicked it into the parking lot, and walked back into the building. I checked my makeup in the mirror on my wall and was reapplying my lipstick when Shawn came over the intercom.

"Miss Price," he said, a smile in his voice, "Mr. Roberts is here."

I slipped my lipstick into my blazer pocket and walked to the door. I turned on a smile. Opening the door, I was taken back. He was handsome. Light-skinned with locs down his back. He was a teddy bear of a man standing almost six-feet tall, maybe about five-nine. He was flashing a smile that lit his whole face up. I could easily see why he was as successful as he was.

"Mr. Blowemup," I said addressing him by his promoter title. "It's so nice to meet you. I'm..."

"Sheila Price, the Queen of Gump Town Night Life," he said, his voice making me tingle.

I blushed.

"I don't know about all that. But I do think we could make some real noise if we partnered. Care to share the throne with me?" I asked.

Shawn laughed under his breath. I blushed again realizing I'd just flirted with the man.

*What the fuck, Sheila? Get it together, girl.*

"I'd certainly consider it," he flirted back.

"Well follow me and let's talk about it," I said leading the way into my office.

Shawn smiled at me when I turned to close the door.

"Cut it out," I mouthed grinning at him.

"So," I started, turning around to find him still standing and looking me up and down. "Well, have a seat," I said, blushing again.

He sat down and I walked back to my seat.

"I've got all the details spelled out for you here, take a moment to look it over," I motioned towards the folder that was sitting in front of him.

"Miss Price... can I call you Sheila?" he asked.

"Yes, please do."

"I'm gonna be honest with you. I've done my research and you're the best in the business. Your name is ringing in these streets and that speaks volumes. Meeting you in person was just a formality and I have to say I'm glad I did," he said, flashing a huge smile that vibrated through me.

"I'm glad you did, too," I said feeling silly for flirting in a business meeting.

"I'd like to invite you out with me Friday night. I've been given a VIP table at 50/50 and would love to let you see me in my element," he offered.

"Sure," I agreed, trying to hide my excitement.

"Ok. Well I'll look over the paperwork and get it back to you as soon as possible. Maybe we could have dinner tonight to celebrate this union and our inevitable takeover."

"So, you're blackmailing me?" I joked.

"Maybe," he said, laughing. "Let's just say I don't want to wait 'til Friday to spend more time with you. I was impressed by your résumé. But seeing you in person, feeling your energy, I have to say you're a beautiful woman. I'd like to get to know you better."

I blushed again.

"I'd love to have dinner with you," I said standing up to escort him to the door. "Make sure you bring those papers with you, though."

"Maybe I will. Maybe I won't. If I have a memory lapse tonight, it may motivate you to meet me for lunch tomorrow... dinner the next day... hell, I can keep this going for as long as it takes," he grinned.

"As long as it takes to what," I said, faking insult.

"To make you my Queen," he said with the most serious face I'd seen on a man in a while.

"You don't have to hold my paperwork hostage to work towards that. Just be who you portray yourself to be and I could see us sharing the throne, like I mentioned before," I laughed looking into his eyes. I had to admit I found his boldness appealing.

"I don't mean just on a business level, Sheila," he made sure I got his meaning.

"Neither do I," I smiled so that he knew I was on the same page.

"Well, I'll see you this evening, then."

"I'll call you to see where we're meeting."

"I'll be listening for your call," he said smiling broadly again before leaving the office.

I watched him walk away and Shawn burst into laughter snatching me out of my daze.

"I assume that went well," he laughed.

"Yeah, it did. He'll have the paperwork signed for me tonight."

"Tonight?" Shawn asked raising an eyebrow.

"Yes, tonight. He asked me to dinner. Am I crazy for accepting a date from someone I'm about to be working with?"

"Sheila, people do it all the time. And it's just dinner, not a marriage proposal. If it goes well, at least you'll know you're with someone on the same page as you."

"What's that supposed to mean?" I asked trying not to be offended.

"Anthony wasn't on your level. I really feel like he was using you. I kept it to myself because I didn't want to overstep my boundaries. If things work with you and Mr. Roberts at least you know he's in your arena. He'll understand what you're working towards. The two of you can help one another grow."

"Interesting," I said smiling at the thought and appreciating his honesty. "Thank you, Shawn. Your honesty is very much appreciated."

I placed my hand on his shoulder appreciatively before walking into my office. I called Ty to make sure that he was on his way to meet me and Tanisha for lunch. I didn't want to face her alone.

*****

"Hey Nel, I'm on the way. Is she there yet?" Tyrone asked me. I could barely hear him over the Jeezy he was blasting.

"Yeah, she's here," I said, dryly. "I made her ass stay up there at reception. I don't need her ratchet ass embarrassing me up here at my place of business."

"Nel, she's still our mom. Show some respect," he said laughing. "And stop ballin' your face up."

I laughed at how well my brother knew me.

"Fine," I huffed. "Just hurry yo' ass up. I wanna get this shit over with."

"I'm turning in now."

"Aight, bye." I hung up the phone.

"Shawn, I'm headed to lunch," I informed him walking out of my office. "Thank you, again, for an excellent job on that offer."

"My pleasure, Sheila. Thank you for believing in me. You've always been really good to me," he smiled. "Good luck on your lunch," he shouted behind me.

I looked back with a nervous smile.

*I'm gonna need luck*, I thought to myself.

I put on a fake smile and walked to the front of the building. I slowed my stride when I saw the way she looked at Tyrone. He'd walked in with a smile and tried to hug her. She stepped back and looked at him like he disgusted her. My face started burning. I picked my speed back up and went to defend my brother.

"What's goin' on here?" I asked walking up and surprising Tanisha.

She turned around with a fake smile plastered on her face.

"Nel! Hey baby! I didn't know your brother was joining us," she said loudly. The way she said 'brother' hurt.

"Use your inside voice and Tyrone is your child, too, so why wouldn't he want to see you since you've chosen to resurface?"

"Hmmph," she grunted. "I just want to see you, my *successful* child. I didn't know I had to entertain a felon just to be in your company," she said arrogantly.

"Look Tanisha. I don't know who the fuck you think you are, but my success is largely due to Ty. You abandoned us *both* so how we turned out is partially due to that abandonment. Tyrone is the only reason I'm even here for this damn lunch. So you're going to show some respect or you can take your ass back to where the hell you came from," I said curtly.

Tanisha rolled her eyes at Tyrone then at me. She seemed to be considering leaving, which would have been fine with me.

"So, where are we eatin'?" she asked conceding.

"Let's go to Kabuki Grill," I suggested. "I'm in the mood for sushi."

"I hope sushi ain't all they got," Tanisha said frowning as we walked through the door Ty was holding open for us.

"No, that's not all they have," I said looking back at Tyrone and rolling my eyes.

"Want me to drive?" Ty asked.

"Yes, please," I agreed.

Tyrone hit the alarm on his Audi. I laughed because the top was still down. I laughed even harder at the look on Tanisha's face when she saw what Tyrone was driving.

"What kinda illegal shit you into to be able to afford this, boy?" she asked standing on the sidewalk watching us get into the car.

"You comin' or not?" Tyrone asked.

I could tell he was getting tired of her shit. She walked up and got into the car.

"A woman must be payin' the note for this thing. You gotta sugar mama, don't you? I guess you are my child." she laughed at her own joke.

Tyrone and I exchanged a look. We both realized that this was probably a mistake. Since it was too late to turn back, I nodded at him letting him know we might as well get it over with.

"How's Tammy?" I asked.

"She's ok. I'm gonna take her pain meds to her when I leave y'all. She's stubborn as hell. Doesn't want me to help her with anything," he said smiling and shaking his head.

"So, you took her to my house and she's all settled in?" I asked.

"Ummm no. She's at my place," he stuttered. "We went to her apartment and saw Scooter's car out there. We didn't know if he was lookin' for somethin' or if his girl had told him Tammy had been discharged and he was lookin' for her. I ain't feel safe takin' her to your house 'cause he knows where you stay so I took her to my house."

"And how does *Samantha* feel about that?"

"She wasn't there when we got there but I ain't too worried about her," Tyrone said dismissively, letting me know that the discussion ended there.

I touched his hand to let him know his message was received.

"So Scooter was over there, huh?" I revisited that little bit of information.

"Yeah, I went back and took care of that before I came over here, though," he explained, making my heart skip a beat.

"Took care of it? Ty, what did you *do*?" I was afraid of the answer.

"Yeah, I called the cops and told 'em it was a break-in. I had to get that nigga off the streets, especially if he got malice in his heart. I gotta protect my girls," he said smiling as he pulled into Kabuki's parking lot.

"So he's locked up?"

"I stayed and watched 'em cart his ass away. Now Tre's ass will have a friend in there."

"Yeah, but they could be in there plottin' too. So be careful, ok," I begged him.

"I ain't worried," he said.

"This place is nice," Tanisha interrupted our conversation.

I'd completely forgotten she was in the car. We all walked into the restaurant and waited to be seated. No one said a word even when the waitress took us to our seats and took our drink orders.

"So, how can I help you?" I asked Tanisha.

"This ain't no business meeting, Penelope, this is lunch with your mother."

"Birth mother," I corrected her, "you didn't raise me. Now, to word my question differently, what do you want Tanisha?"

"I was hoping to get to know you. I saw the write-up on you in RSVP Montgomery and am so proud of how you turned out. I wanna be in your life and in my grandson's life," she explained.

"But not in Tyrone's? He's got twins on the way."

"Oh really," she said, shooting a nasty look at Ty. "Congratulations," she said, dryly.

The waitress brought out our drinks and took our orders. I waited until she left before saying anything else.

"Look, Tanisha, you got one more time to be nasty to my brother and your ass will be lookin' for a ride back to whatever hell hole you dragged yourself out of. You've got some nerve tryna judge some fuckin' body. Do you remember that you were a crack whore? Do you know how many times my brother was violated to keep them nasty ass men you were fuckin' off of me? Do you remember fuckin' your own son when nobody wanted that crusty wore-out pussy of yours?"

"Nel!" Tyrone yelled my name stopping me tantrum.

"What Ty? She's still our mother? Is that what you're about to say? All she did was give birth to us. You fed me. You took care of me! It's because of her we were separated! You ended up in that fuckin' filthy ass group home. I was lucky I didn't end up in a fucked up foster home where I needed your protection and you weren't there. I'm lucky I ended up somewhere I was loved. But she wants to bring her ass back around twenty damn years later and act like she better than somebody. Bitch needs a reality check."

Tyrone looked around at the people who had stopped their meals to watch the spectacle I was making of myself. Tanisha was searching the floor for something. She couldn't look me in the face. I looked around, suddenly remembering where I was and who I was and embarrassed by my actions. I'd lost control but she'd really pushed my buttons. There are a few things I don't play about and my brother was one of them. I'd beat a brick and put a rock in the hospital for Tyrone Karlisle Price.

"Nel, calm down," Tyrone said, his face red with embarrassment.

"I'm sorry, Ty, she just pissed me the fuck off," I said softly.

When the waitress brought our food, she avoided making eye contact with me, too. I'd really made an ass of myself but I was gonna eat my food and get the hell outta that place. I'd waited my whole life to read Tanisha's ass and I'm glad I got the chance, even if I did embarrass myself in the process.

We all ate, not saying anything. Tyrone kept looking at me to make sure I was okay. I was worried about him being ok. All that shit she'd said had to hurt to hear. I really felt bad for him. When I was paying the check, Tanisha finally decided to open her mouth.

"Penelope," she said, her voice making me cringe.

"Yes," I answered not really caring what she had to say.

"I love you. I love you, too, Tyrone. I was a terrible mother. Them drugs had my brain fried, but I spent the last five years in prison getting clean and wishin' I had been there for y'all. Tyrone, I'm not angry with you, baby," she said, reaching for his hand and looking him in the eyes.

Tyrone took her hand and squeezed it.

"I just look at you and know that everything that happened to you was my fault. The things I did to you were..." she paused, "just nasty. I'm so sorry, son. You never got to be a child but now I look at the man you are, despite everything you went through, and I'm embarrassed because I know you did all of it in spite of me and going to prison."

I looked at Tyrone and saw his face wet with tears. My brother had waited decades for that apology. I saw the little boy with the busted lip and black eye who fought to keep our groceries from being stolen flash through his eyes. I could hear my heart thudding in my ears.

"I've been in and outta jail," Tanisha explained. After they took y'all I spiraled out of control. I almost killed myself tryin' to smoke and fuck the pain away. I came lookin' for y'all 'cause I was diagnosed with AIDS and the only people I needed to make amends with was y'all."

"Oh momma," I said feeling tears in my eyes.

"But I ain't come here for a pity party or to ask y'all for money or nothin'. I just need y'alls forgiveness before I leave this earth," she said, reaching for my hand.

"I forgive you, momma," Tyrone said without hesitation.

"I forgive you," I said not really sure if I meant it.

"Sheila Penelope Price, don't lie to me," she threatened, "you know I know when you lyin'."

"Well, momma, ... Tanisha, I've just gotta lot of my own shit goin' on right now, so I don't know if I have it in me to forgive you or anyone else right now. I gotta cancer diagnosis last week, so you catchin' something I feel like you did to yourself versus me gettin' somethin' I don't deserve makes it hard for me to have any kinda sympathy for you," I said honestly.

The waitress brought my card and the receipts back. I left her a fifty dollar tip because of all the trouble I had caused and got up to leave. Tyrone sat there staring at me like he was made of stone.

"Nel, when were you gonna tell me?" he asked looking like I'd just spit in his face.

"When I got the definite diagnosis. That day I saw you and Samantha at the doctor's office, they'd called me in to tell me they'd found cancerous cells. But mad at Anthony because I saw him fuckin Delilah, I went and had an abortion. So they can't run any tests until I'm cleared by my gynecologist. So, I didn't see the point in saying anything until I knew what I was telling, ya know," I tried to explain while leading the way to the door. I was *beyond* ready to go.

"This has been one hell of a week," Tyrone said as we got in his car.

I laughed, realizing it'd been a hell of a couple of weeks. I truly needed a vacation. When we got back to my job Tyrone cut the car off but none of us moved.

"I don't know how much time I got left," Tanisha said, "but I'd love to meet my grandson and hope to be around to meet my grand-twins," she said smiling.

"Let's start slow," I said. "I don't want you coming into Jeffrey's life just to disappear like you did with us. My foster mom is the grandmother he knows and I'm not gonna uproot that just because you have a case of conscience."

"Well, let's keep in touch and maybe spend more time getting acquainted. I wanna get to know you... both of you," she said looking from me to Tyrone.

"Ok," Tyrone smiled. We both gave her our business cards and she wrote her number down for us. We all got out of the car and shared hugs before going our separate ways. I walked back into the office smiling broadly, something I definitely hadn't expected.

## Tyrone

It had been a hell of a week, and it only seemed to be getting crazier for me. Here I was leaving the mother of my unborn children seething mad in my apartment when all I'd wanted a week ago, hell, a matter of days ago was for her to be there with me. I dreamt of us being a family and then Tammy got shot and nothing else seemed to matter. I wanted to snap that nigga Tre's neck when that shit happened. It had taken all of my self-control not to take Scooter's ass out, too, when I went back to Tammy's apartment and found him there. But all I could do was think of my children, of Nel, and of Tammy. Even though they'd be worth every second of a life sentence that nigga wasn't worth the trouble. So I called the cops and they caught his ass breaking and entering. They probably got his ass for tampering with a crime scene, too. And there was no tellin' what illegal shit he had on him, especially if he was there to kill Tammy like she thought he was.

Then, after that lunch with my birth mother that started off terribly but ended on a much better note, I realized that life was too short. I love Sam, but I'm in love with Tammy and now that the opportunity was presenting itself I didn't want to miss out on it. Sam was still married and I didn't trust her because she'd been sneaking off and acting kinda strange lately. I felt like she was fuckin' Anthony. And with *my* babies inside of her. At least she said they were my babies.

"Tyrone, you've lost your mind you know that, right," Tammy said bringing me out of my own head.

"Why you say that?" I asked her even though I knew what she was talking about.

"Dude, Sam gone kill your ass in your sleep. Fuckin' wit' that girl while she pregnant and shit. I don't know what the hell you're thinkin'," she said shaking her head.

"Sam ain't gone do shit," I laughed at the thought.

"Ty baby, the woman had death in her eyes when she was blockin' that door. I know that look. I saw it a thousand times with Tre. That's dangerous," she said with seriousness in her tone.

"You're worryin' for nothin', baby." I laid my hand on her thigh.

"Alright, watch that hand," she joked trying to lighten the mood.

"And what if I don't?" I asked sliding my hand further up her thigh.

"Ty, stop," she whined but made no efforts to move my hand.

I took that as a green light and kept inching up her thigh untiled I reached her hip. I eased my hand between her legs and massaged her pussy through her pants.

"Mmm baby," she moaned moving her hips in motion with my massage.

I turned into the alley behind my sister's house, never missing a beat with my massage. I put the car in park and leaned over, kissing her passionately. I trailed my kisses down her neck, massaging her even harder. She moaned while I sucked on her neck.

I used my free hand to lift her shirt and pull out her breast. I took it into my mouth rolling my tongue around her nipple. I was rock hard and wanted to feel her so bad it was starting to hurt.

"Ty," she moaned loudly, "I want it."

I took my cue and stopped massaging her. I jumped out of the car and ran around, opening her door. I scooped Tammy out of her seat, carrying her to the door and unlocking it without putting her down. I carried her to the couch and laid her down gently, pulling up her shirt and giving each of her breasts equal attention. She was pulling her pants off while she squealed in pleasure.

"Baby, please," she begged.

I stopped sucking on her breasts and pulled my sweatpants down. My dick jumped free, rock hard and throbbing. She sat up and took me into her mouth. She slurped and sucked me until I was weak in the knees. I stepped back, pulling my dick out of her mouth. She was sucking so hard it made a popping sound when it came out.

"Are you sure you're ready to do this?" I asked, massaging myself, but with a very serious look on my face.

"Yes," she said smiling at me, "it feels like I've been waiting for it my whole life."

I eased on top of her making sure to support my weight and not fall on her arm, and slid inside of her. It felt so good I almost lost my composure. I stroked her slow so she could feel all of me. So that she could feel all of the years I'd been in love with her. My heartbeat was in every stroke.

"Tammy, I want you to be mine," I said staring into her beautiful face.

"But Sam..."

I leaned in and silenced her with a kiss. I kept stroking, feeling her breath release into my mouth in time with my motions. I leaned down so that my lips were against her ear.

"Tre's gone. Sam will be, too. I want us to be together. Come live with me. Let's do what we've dreamt about for years."

"Are... you... for... real," she asked not believing her ears.

"Dead assed," I said while making love to her.

"Then yes! Yes, baby!" she screamed in orgasm.

I took my groove to a whole other level. I wanted to touch her soul. Become one with her. I needed her to feel just how serious I was.

"I love you, Tammy," I said, hitting her bottom and squirting my seed as deep inside of her as I possibly could.

If she could have children, I'd spend the rest of my life filling her with my babies.

"I love you, too, Tyrone," she said, shaking again.

I raised up and found her with tears streaming down her face. I got worried because I thought I'd hurt her arm.

"Baby, what's wrong? Did I hurt you?" I asked panicking.

"No," she said sniffling, "I just never thought this day would come. I wish I could give you babies. Then it would be perfect."

"It *is* perfect baby," I said trying to ease her mind. "If I never had a child, I would be content as long as I have you."

I got up and sat on the edge of the couch. I had to figure out how to break it to Sam. I didn't want to be cut out of my kids' lives. I wasn't worried about her cutting her money off. I didn't want to hurt her either, though. We'd been dealin' for over a year so I had to take her feelings into consideration, too.

"You thinkin' 'bout how to break it to Sam, huh?" Tammy read my mind.

"I'm thinking about a lot of things," I confessed, "but yeah, that's one of the most pressing things right now."

"Look baby," Tammy said sitting up beside me, "there's no rush. I don't expect the shit to happen overnight. I know y'all got history and now there are babies involved. I'm patient. I've waited all this time. If you mean it when you say that you wanna be with me, then I can wait 'til you can tie up some loose ends," she said looking me square in the eyes.

"I promise you won't have to wait long. I want us to be together," I said meaning every word.

I got dressed and went out to the car to get her things. I hated that she was staying with Nel instead of me. I wanted to be the one taking care of her. I'd just have to be here as often as I could. When I walked back into the house, Tammy was fast asleep.

I picked her up, took her to the spare bedroom, laid her down, and covered her up. I picked up her clothes and brought her bags back there, too. I was unpacking her things when I heard the alarm chime.

"Hello?" Nel yelled into the house.

I walked out of the room and into the living room.

"Hey Nel," I said kissing her on the cheek.

"Where's Tammy? I got us some take-out from Chili's."

"She sleep."

"Oh, ok. I'll just put hers in the fridge. You hungry? We can share mine. I'm goin' to dinner tonight, so I probably won't eat all this."

"Dinner?" I asked raising an eyebrow. "With who?"

"Yeah, it's kind of a working dinner. The promoter I was meeting today wants to meet for dinner. He's bringing the signed paperwork."

"He can't bring it to your job tomorrow?" I asked protectively.

"He could but I kinda wanna see him, too," she confessed.

"Oh really," I grinned, "you sure you ready for that? The Anthony thing is still pretty fresh."

"Yes Ty," she said, rolling her eyes. "I don't want to sit here moping about someone else's husband. I'm not saying I'm tryna date the man, or even fuck him. It'll just be nice to be in the company of somebody who wants my company, ya know?"

"Ok, just take your time and be careful," I said hoping this dude wasn't on no bullshit.

"Yes, Daddy," she said sarcastically.

"Well, I'mma go get some clothes, then, and stay with Tammy and Jeff tonight since you're goin' out," I said, heading for the door.

"It's just gonna be you and Tammy. Jeff's stayin' at my foster mom's tonight. *Oh shit*," she said like she'd just remembered something.

She walked out of the kitchen and into her bedroom to make a phone call. I headed towards the door. Sam and I needed to talk about a few things before I came back here.

"Be back, Nel," I yelled before I left headed home. I got a feeling in my gut that this was going to be an interesting encounter.

# Samantha

I know Tyrone better bring his ass back here, swellin' up on me and shit so he can take that hoe to his sister's house. Tyrone is *my* man and he'd lost his damn mind. But I had every intention on helping his ass find it!

I sat on the foot of the bed, flipping through the channels on the TV. I got angrier and angrier with every channel. I was .38 hot by the time I heard the door open. I flew down the hallway. We were gonna get some straightenin' *right now*.

"Tyrone, we need to talk," I said, almost all the way in his face.

"You're right, we do," he said calmly.

He walked past me into the kitchen and poured himself a shot of Petrón. He walked back to the living room and sat down in the arm chair, bottle in hand.

"Tyrone, you disrespected the fuck outta me today. I pay the bills in this house and the note on that car you had that bitch in," I said, still standing with my hands on my hips.

"So stop payin' 'em," he said, taking his shot and pouring himself another.

I stared at him in disbelief. What in the hell was wrong with him?

"So it's that simple for you, huh? I guess you've made your decision and me, these babies, and all this time we've had together mean nothing to you!"

"I didn't say any of that," he said taking the shot he'd just poured. "You're putting words in my mouth. All I said was stop paying the rent and car note."

His calm frustrated the fuck out of me. I wanted to bust him over the head with that bottle.

"So what does this mean for us, Tyrone?" I asked through clenched teeth.

"Sam, have a seat. You said you wanted to talk but it seems to me like you wanna argue. I'm not in the mood to argue. I've had a long fucking day and just want to have a discussion like grown folks," he said looking at me in a way I'd never seen him look at me before.

I walked over to the couch and had a seat facing him.

"Okay, well talk," I said crossing my hands over my belly.

"Samantha, let's be real. When I met you, you were married. A year later, you're still married. I never expected you to leave your husband for me and I sure as hell didn't expect you to get pregnant," he said.

"So now you don't want the babies?" I asked, my eyes wild.

"Again, not what I said. I'm excited about the twins and I really do love you but I would be stupid to see this as anything other than what it is," he rationalized.

"But I got the papers drawn up. And we've got this vacation planned with the kids," I said crying.

"Did you sign them? Did he?" he asked making me look to the floor.

"Not yet, but..." I started to explain.

"So why don't you and your husband take your children on vacation. I love you but I'm not blind or crazy. Y'all got a lot of love and a lot of history. Maybe y'all just need a change of scenery."

"Are you serious, Tyrone? So you just gonna cut me off like that? What about the twins?" I asked, devastated.

"I told you, I'm excited about the twins and we can co-parent. I'm going to ask for a paternity test because like I said, I'm not stupid," he said, taking another shot.

I felt like I'd just been slapped in the face. I stood up and rushed across the room. I swung and slapped the shit out of him.

"I know that Tammy bitch put you up to this shit," I said, slapping him again, "you were happy until that bitch came around here. I *knew* she wanted you!"

I swung again, but he caught my hand. I managed to pop him one more good time before he caught that hand, too, and stood up out of his seat.

"Woman you done lost every bit of your mind laying your fucking hands on me. I think you need to leave before somebody gets hurt."

I raised my foot and kicked him in his nuts. He let me go and fell back into the chair, groaning.

"Fuck you, Tyrone. You can't hurt me no more. I'm gone. And I'm taking these babies with me. Let DHR give you your goddamn paternity test. And we'll see how long you can afford this apartment and that car once they tap that ass with child support. Leaving me for that old ratchet ass, sterile ass, trap house hoe," I said picking up my keys and purse and heading for the door before he could get up.

I slammed the door behind me and got in my car to go home. My mama always said, "The hell you know is better than the hell you don't know."

# Anthony

Beth lay sleeping in my arms, her fat ass rubbing against my dick. I didn't even get aroused. After watching her and Sam together, I wasn't feeling her anymore. I found myself thinking about Sheila. She'd been all mine, never even looked at another man, even when she found out I was married.

Delilah's ass had been fucking all across the city. I could feel when another man had been in her even with her exercises. Hell, she was fucking Beth when she got her stupid ass locked up for jumping on Sheila. Now I find out Sam's been fucking Tyrone for a year. I swear these hoes ain't loyal. None but Sheila.

I slid out of the bed and grabbed my cell phone deciding to give her a call. It went to voicemail so I tried again. Voicemail again. I was about to leave a message when I got a text alert.

**Sheila:** *Getting ready for a date. What's up?*

I felt my ears start ringing. *A date? With who?* I asked myself. The thought of another man making her smile pissed me off. I didn't respond. I put my phone down on the nightstand and rolled Beth over.

I put my face in between her legs and made a feast of her until she nutted all on my face. I climbed on top of her and let her lick her juices off of my face. I took her legs and placed them on my shoulders, leaning forward so that her toes were touching the bed on either side of her head.

I pushed myself into her tight, wet pussy and fucked her until I felt better about Sheila bein' on a date. I made her scream until she was hoarse, fuckin' her like I'd never fucked anyone before. As much as she begged for me to stop, she kept cumming. Her pussy muscles flexed, gripping my dick, every time she came. When I came, I pulled out, panting, and rolled over to go to sleep.

I didn't wanna hold her. All I could do was think of how Sheila would cuddle up under me and I'd melt into her softness. How even when I was out doin' my dirt I knew she was there waiting for me. I wasn't worried about who she may have been with because from the moment we became official, she'd centered her life around me. I thought about picking my phone up and calling her but I knew she didn't want to talk to me. And I couldn't blame her. Sheila was the kind of woman most men would die to lay beside every night. But I'd treated her like just another hoe I was fuckin'.

I eased outta bed and walked into the kitchen. The divorce papers were still on the table. I picked up the pen that Sam had brought along with hers and signed my name everywhere it asked for it. Then I walked over to the couch and laid down. If I wanted Sheila, I was gonna have to get my shit together. When I came to her I wanted to make sure I came correct and ready for commitment.

*****

I woke up from my nap with a crook in my neck and a warmth on my dick. I looked down to find Beth with her lips wrapped around my dick. I'd thought I was dreaming but I wasn't. I looked at her and my dick lost its erection. As good as it felt and as much as I hated the reality that being with Sheila exclusively meant I'd probably never get head again, I didn't want any kind of sex from anyone else.

I sat up and pushed Beth away by her forehand. She looked like I'd just hit her in the face.

"What the fuck?" she asked, her voice a high-pitched squeal.

"I'm not in the mood," I said honestly.

"That's not what ya dick says," she said flirtatiously.

"I'm the brains of this operation. He ain't callin' no shots around here," I said, sarcasm in my tone.

"Well then, can I get some head? I'm excited. Help me out, baby," she pouted.

"Not my problem. Don't you have some toys at home that'll help you fix that?" I asked, getting up and going into the bathroom to take a piss.

I turned on the shower. I knew it was just my conscience but I felt dirty. I needed a shower. Beth came stomping into the bathroom, her face beet red.

"So you're puttin' me out? I fuck you and then come sleep with your wife and you send me home to go fuck myself?" she asked, screaming.

"Nobody told you to bring your ass over here. That was your choice. And if my memory serves me right, you were more than willing to let me up in that pussy. So go play victim somewhere else," I snapped, shaking the last drops of pee before flushing and stepping into the shower.

"Fuck you, Anthony! You'll regret this," Beth said.

I heard her stomp out of the bathroom, muttering under her breath. I started rubbing the bar of soap all over me, hoping her crazy ass would be gone when I got out of the shower. I wasn't too worried about her threats. My baby mamas were from Tulane Court and Samantha was from Tuskegee. You ain't seen mad until you've pissed one of them off. I figured she'd tear up some shit in the house, maybe slash my tires and be done with it.

When I got out of the shower, I walked into my bedroom expecting the worst. I was surprised to find my house unbothered. I walked through the kitchen and out into the garage to look at my car. It was fine, too.

"Man, that bitch was bluffin'. She was just in her feelings," I said, adjusting my towel and walking back into the house to relax and enjoy my peace.

I watched a few flicks, got myself off, and then took a nap. I woke up and the clock told me that I'd been asleep for two hours. I needed to get dressed because the kids would be home soon. I was pulling my Polo over my head when there was a knock on my front door. I wasn't expecting anyone so I walked to the door cautiously.

"Who is it?" I asked.

"Police!" the officer answered.

Concerned, I opened the door. There were two male officers, both about six feet in height, standing on the other side of the screen door.

"Can I help you?" I asked, not opening the screen door. I needed that barrier between us.

"Sir, do you know an Elizabeth Henry?" he asked with a serious look on his face.

"Yes, I do. What's going on? Is she ok?" I asked, worried that the crazy bitch had done something to herself. But if she had, I wouldn't be the one the cops came to see.

"Well, Miss Henry has accused you of sexual assault and we have a warrant for your arrest."

"Sexual assault? You mean *rape*? No, you've got the wrong person. Who are you looking for?" I asked, knowing that they *had* to be wrong.

"Are you Anthony Bailey?" the officer asked.

"Yes I am, but I didn't rape nobody."

"Well, sir, Miss Henry said you did. We're collecting a rape kit now and need you to come with us for questioning and a DNA sample."

I couldn't believe my ears. Of all the psycho bitches to stick my dick in, I'd chosen one who accused me of rape because I put her ass out without helping her get a nut! And of course they were gonna find my DNA in her, I'd fucked her today. This bitch just pulled a Monica Lewinski on me.

"Let me get my keys and lock up my house," I said, a pained look on my face.

I walked over to the table by the door and grabbed my keys. I locked the door, walked out of the house, and was handcuffed and escorted to the police car.

I saw Andrea pull up with my children in the car as my head was being lowered into the back seat. She hopped out of the car before it had stopped moving and ran over to the police cruiser.

"What's going on?" she asked, frantically.

"Just call Sam and tell her Beth is accusing me of rape. She'll know what I'm talking about. Take my kids to your house for me."

"Ok," Andrea said, frowning.

The words 'I told you so' were plastered on her face. She ran back to her car and pulled out her cell phone. As bad as this situation was, my children seeing me being driven off in a police car was worse. My eyes filled with tears when I saw Sarabi mouth the word 'daddy' and begin to cry. I wanted to wring Beth's fuckin' neck but it was all my fault. I shouldn't have been fuckin' with her in the first place.

# Sheila

Today had started out pretty shitty but I was really happy with how things had turned out. I had a date tonight that was doubling as the start of a great business relationship. But I couldn't help but worry about whether it was a bad look to be dating this man. All this time I'd managed to keep my name clean and maintain my respect in this male-dominated profession because I'd never slept with any of my promoters or any of the club owners. That was what set me apart from the rest.

I wasn't trying to tarnish my reputation on a rebound fling. On the way home, I pondered the decision. I mean, looking at my track record with Tre, then Anthony and Delilah, I wasn't the best judge of character when it came to relationships. And what if he just wanted to use me to break into the scene here? I felt so lost. I'd never been the distrustful sort. I always gave people the benefit of the doubt, but after recent events I wondered if it wasn't better for me to make people earn my trust.

I decided to go on the date but make it clear that I wasn't easy. We could go out as friends, but it would take some work to get me to be his. I needed time to get over Anthony, too. He wasn't about shit but I still loved him. I sighed as that reality set in. I pulled into my driveway and saw Tyrone's car. I got excited because I could ask Tammy what she thought.

"Hello?" I yelled, walking into the house.

Tyrone came flying around the corner from my spare bedroom, meeting me in the living room.

"Hey Nel," he said, kissing me on the cheek.

"Where's Tammy? I got us some takeout from Chili's?" I asked.

"She sleep," he informed me.

"Oh ok. I'll just put hers in the fridge. You hungry? We can share mine. I'm goin' to dinner tonight, so I probably won't eat all this."

"*Dinner?*" he asked, raising an eyebrow, "*With whom?*"

"Yeah, it's kind of a working dinner. The promoter I was meeting today wants to meet for dinner. He's bringing the signed paperwork."

"He can't bring it to your job tomorrow?" Ty asked protectively.

"He could, but I kinda wanna see him, too," I confessed, blushing.

"Oh really," he said, grinning, "You sure you ready for that? The Anthony thing is still pretty fresh."

"Yes, Ty," I said, rolling my eyes. "I don't want to sit here moping about someone else's husband. I'm not saying I'm tryna date the man, or even fuck him. It'll just be nice to be in the company of somebody who wants my company, ya know?"

"Ok, just take your time and be careful," he said, his tone skeptical.

"Yes, Daddy," I said, sarcastically.

"Well, I'mma go get some clothes, then, and stay with Tammy and Jeff tonight since you're goin' out," he said, heading for the door.

"It's just gonna be you and Tammy. Jeff's stayin' at my foster mom's tonight. *Oh shit*," I said, suddenly remembering dinner with my foster mom.

I ran out of the kitchen and into my bedroom, to call her and see if I could just stop by there to talk before my date.

"Hey Ma," I said when she answered the phone. "I know I was coming over for dinner but I just scheduled a dinner meeting for tonight."

"All work and no play," she said laughing.

"I know, Ma," I felt guilty.

I should've rescheduled my date but I didn't want to.

"Well, you gonna stop by on your way to your meeting? You said we need to talk," she said, sounding concerned.

"Yes ma'am," I agreed, but then thought twice about telling her about my cancer diagnosis. "But Ma, it's really nothing serious."

"So you were just trying to get some meatloaf outta me, huh?" she teased, "and now you're not coming to eat it with me."

"Awww momma, don't do that," I reconsidered cancelling my date.

"I'm just teasin' you, child," she laughed into the phone again, "just come over tomorrow and we'll catch up over leftovers. If that man child of yours leaves any, that is."

This time I laughed with her because Jeffrey had become a garbage disposal. That child could eat.

"Let's just hope the child doesn't eat a whole meatloaf," I said. "I'll definitely be by there tomorrow, not meetings, no interruptions. I promise."

"Ok Nel, love you."

"Love you, too, momma."

I walked back out of my room to find that Tyrone hadn't made it back from packing some clothes so I went to check up on Tammy. I went into the spare room, expecting to find her asleep. I was shocked to find her stubborn ass unpacking her bags.

"Girl, you just won't sit yo' ass still, huh?" I asked, startling her.

"I can't just lay around doin' nothin', chile."

I walked on into the room shaking my head, and started helping her to unpack.

"Did you get some rest at Ty's house today at least?" I asked, putting her clothes on hangers.

"Not for real," Tammy said with a sigh. "Between wondering what the hell Scooter was doin' at my house to Sam's angry ass giving me her "the boy is mine" routine, I've had too much shit goin' on to get much rest, ya know," she said sitting down on the bed.

"Well, Ty called the cops on Scooter, said he saw them carrying his ass off downtown," I told her trying to ease her mind.

"Oh yeah? Well, that's cool. We didn't really get to talk much when he got back because Sam was there," she said, sounding relieved and annoyed all at once.

"So Sam came pissin' on trees, huh?"

"Yeah, she tried it but you know that bitch don't intimidate shit over here."

"Ooh, somebody's claws are out. Tammy, what's the deal with you and my brother? Like, are y'all gonna be together?" I asked.

"Girl, I don't know. I mean, the shit with Tre is still fresh and Sam is fuckin' pregnant so this shit is complicated. She ain't gonna let him go anytime soon," she said.

"Yeah, especially since she gave Anthony the divorce papers," I added.

"Real shit?" I asked, her face wrinkling up.

"Real shit," I confirmed. "I wonder if Ty knows because he didn't say anything when we had lunch with our birth mother."

"Your who?" Tammy asked, coming out of her feelings.

"Yeah, she went to my foster mom's looking for me last night and then showed up at my job this morning. I was finna write her ass a check and send her back to the pits of hell that she dragged herself out of. But Ty talked me into having lunch with her."

"How'd that go?"

"Pretty well, actually, after I read her ass for bein' disrespectful to my brother. She told us she has AIDS and wants to spend what time she has left getting to know us."

"That's so sad. I'm sorry, Nel."

"It's fine. I figured her ass was dead somewhere anyway. At least she's trying though, so I'm gonna let that count for something," I said.

I checked my watch, not wanting to talk about her anymore. I had to make a call to find out where my date was gonna be.

"Got somewhere to go?" she asked, raising an eyebrow.

"Kinda. That promoter I met with today asked me out on a date this evening. I need to call him and see where we're meeting and what time," I confessed.

"Look at you! Back on the horse, huh?" Tammy teased.

I blushed, not knowing if that was a good thing or a bad thing.

"I don't know, Tam. I mean he seems cool but I've still got these Anthony feelings to sort out and my reputation to consider. I don't date or fuck around with promoters and club owners and shit because I don't want to be accused of fuckin' my way to the top, you know?"

"But, Nel, you're already on the top, hun. Your rep ain't gonna be tarnished by gettin' to know this dude. Unless you're planning on fuckin' him tonight," she said, smiling.

I stopped hanging up her clothes and sat down beside her on the bed. I must have had a guilty look on my face because she burst out laughing. I smiled at her.

"Tam, being honest, I'd fuck him six ways to Sunday. But he seems like someone I could actually build with."

"Oh," she said, finally understanding my dilemma. "Well, just get to know him. You never know what could happen. At least you two are in the same profession so you're kind of on the same page," she said.

"Now you sound like Shawn," I laughed.

"Well, maybe there's something to it if both of us are saying it. Just give dude a chance and don't hold him accountable for Ant or even Tre's bullshit, ok," she said, giving me a stern look.

I nodded my head in agreement. Getting up to make a call.

"You don't count my brother out, either," I said. "I really think y'all would be great together."

"Speaking of Tyrone, where is he?"

"He went to get some clothes. Apparently, he plans to be here with you when I'm not," I said, giving her a wink.

"He went back to the house? Oh shit," she said, getting up to check her phone. "Sam's probably giving his ass the business as we speak."

"Or he's telling her where his heart is and giving her ass her walking papers. Ty isn't really a fan of women giving him the business," I pointed out.

"We'll go with that scenario," Tammy blushed. "Do you really think your brother would leave her for me? I mean, I can't give him children or anything," she asked insecurely.

"He doesn't care about that. I've never seen him look at another woman like he does you. Not even Sam. Just trust in his feelings for you," I said before walking away.

I had pep in my step walking back to my room to make the phone call.

"Hello? May I speak with Mr. Blowemup?" I asked when he answered the phone.

"You can call me Ron," he said laughing.

"Ok, Ron," I said, "how are you this evening?"

"I'm well. Excited that you called. I was starting to think I was gonna have to hold these papers hostage until you caved."

"So you're not against blackmail?"

"There's no limit to what I'm willing to do to get what I want."

"Ron, I have to ask you, and I'm being for real, what is it that you want from me?"

"To get to know you. I mean, we're gonna be working together but you're beautiful and I feel like you're someone I could be with. I know you're not the kind to sleep around, like I told you, I did my research. But ass ain't hard to come by, especially in our business. But somebody worth having... now that's hard to come by nowadays."

"Good answer," I teased.

"Was it good enough for you to let me treat you to dinner?"

"Of course," I said, my cheeks hurting from smiling. "Where are we going?"

"It's a surprise. Call me when you're in the car and heading out and I'll text you the address to put in your GPS. Can you be ready by six thirty?"

"A surprise, huh? Yeah, I can be ready at six thirty. I'll call you then."

"See you then," he said. "Bye, beautiful."

I hung up with a smile plastered on my face. I walked into my closet and started throwing dresses onto my bed. I'd get Tammy to help me choose my outfit. I walked out of my room to solicit her assistance when Tyrone burst into the house like somebody had pissed him off.

"Hey Ty, you ok?" I asked, looking at my brother's face.

"That bitch hit me," he said, touching his face.

I could see that his lip was split and his right cheek was red. I felt my face get hot. Sam had lost her whole damn mind puttin' hands on my fuckin' brother.

Tammy must have heard what he'd said, too, because she rounded the corner at full-speed.

"What the fuck?" she said, sitting beside my brother on the couch.

"We need to go see that bitch," I said to Tammy.

"Naw," Ty said to me and Tammy who was nodding her agreement. "I put her out my fuckin' gate and got the main office to change my locks and key code. Outside of my kids, me and Sam ain't got shit to discuss."

"Man, she better hope I don't see her ass," I said, sitting down on the arm of my couch angrily.

"Don't worry about her. Leave her and Anthony where the fuck they at. Karma is a bitch. She's gonna get what's comin' to her. Her fuck ass husband will, too."

We all sat there in silence. We heard what he was saying but Tammy and I shared a look that said the shit wasn't over. Not by a long shot.

# Samantha

I got a call from Andrea just as I was turning into the neighborhood.

"Hey, girl," I answered, "you at my house? I need a drink and an ear."

"Kris just got arrested," Andrea said with panic in her voice.

"What? What for?" I asked, pressing down on the gas pedal.

"I don't know. I was bringing the kids to him and they were putting him in the police car. He told me to call you so you can meet him downtown. Said to tell you that somebody named Beth was accusing him of raping her," she relayed the message.

"Beth? Rape? Seriously?" I said in disbelief. "Ok, how are the kids?" I asked, wanting to make sure they were okay before I turned around and headed downtown.

"They'll be alright. Sarabi is having a fit. It's fucked up that they saw their daddy carted away like that," she said. "You go get my brother. I got them."

"Ok," I said, hanging up.

*I wonder what the fuck Kris and Beth ended up into it about that had her accusing him of rape*, I thought to myself. *I need to leave Tyrone's ass the fuck alone and get my family straight.*

At that moment, I decided I was done with Tyrone Price. He could see his children on a visitation schedule set by the court after he got his paternity test. I drove as fast as my Mustang would take me towards Downtown Montgomery. I knew the bail bondsman was gonna get tired of seeing me after a while. Two times in a week made me reconsider the reality that I had terrible taste in men. Regardless, Kris was my husband and I was gonna stand by him no matter what he'd gotten himself into.

I reached the AAA Bail Bonds office just as they were processing Kris. Steve, the bondsman, confirmed that he'd been arrested for sexual assault. That Beth had come down and signed a warrant on him saying that he'd raped her and the rape kit had revealed his DNA. My head started to hurt. I'd brought this psycho into our house and now my husband was in jail. I didn't know how things had gotten this bad. They were both asleep in the bed together when I'd left. I needed to talk to my husband but was told that he was being held without bond and would have to go before a judge.

I felt like I was experiencing déjà vu. This was Tyrone all over again. I wanted to call Beth and curse her ass out but I knew that could make matters worse. I decided to go home and check on my children. I called my attorney on the way. He asked me to stop by his office so that he could get the full story. I didn't have time for all that. I just needed his ass to go talk to my husband and wanted to make sure he was available to represent him in the morning.

I pulled into the parking lot of the building that housed Winchester and Associates on Carmichael Road. I got out of the car and became immediately embarrassed thinking of what I was going to have to reveal about myself to aid in my husband's defense. The embarrassment got worse when I realized that, just this week, I had met with him to draw up divorce papers for the man I now wanted to pay him to defend.

I sat in the waiting area until I was called back. When I sat down at his desk, Mark Winchester gave me a harsh look.

"Ok, start at the beginning. I thought you were divorcing Mr. Bailey. But now you want to hire me to defend him?" he asked in a no nonsense tone.

"Yes," I confirmed, clearing my throat.

"So, we're not getting divorced now?"

"Not right now. Right now, I need my husband out of jail and this ridiculous case thrown out."

"Ok, why do you say that it's ridiculous? Sexual assault is a very serious accusation," Mr. Winchester stated the obvious.

"I know. And I wouldn't be here if I didn't *know* that my husband didn't rape that woman," I said matter-of-factly.

"And just how do you *know* that?" he asked with a raised eyebrow.

"Because we had sex with her together," I said, blushing with embarrassment.

"Hmmmm," he said, leaning forward, "and when was this?"

"Today," I told him, knowing that I was the only person who could disprove her accusation.

"Sit tight, let me make a call," he said, walking out of the office.

He returned about ten minutes later with a somber look on his face. I prepared myself for the bad news.

"So?" I asked anxiously.

"He goes before the judge tomorrow for his bail hearing then they'll set a date for his trial. I contacted her attorney and she's not denying the threesome, which is good, but she's claiming that the assault happened before that, when she was packing her girlfriend Delilah's things up. She says your husband was present when the locksmith helped her get into her car at Vaughn Road Park. Says that your husband made several sexual advances at her while her car was being unlocked and, in the midst of rejecting him, she informed him that she was going to pack up Delilah's apartment and move them into storage. Your husband offered to help and she declined but he showed up anyway and that's when the assault took place."

"Well," I said, thinking aloud, "the locksmith was probably my brother-in-law Matt, Kris's sister's husband and his business partner. Delilah is in jail for assaulting my husband's girlfriend, Sheila, after not leaving when she was asked to leave the woman's house. And it makes no sense for her to admit to the threesome but then accusing him of assaulting her prior to coming to *his* home to have sex with him and his wife." I went through all of the details he'd given me.

"Interesting," Mr. Winchester said. "Mrs. Johnson, I'm *your* attorney. You haven't hired me to represent your husband just yet, so as your attorney, I have to pose a question to you."

"Ok, shoot."

"You left my office today with divorce papers in your hand. You wanted out of your marriage because of your husband's infidelity. The same infidelity that now has him sitting in jail on a rape charge. But, instead of seeing this as your opportunity to get out of the marriage, you are willing to expose embarrassing details about your marriage and your sex life and hire me to help get him out of jail and plead his case. Is that right?"

I looked at my hands, feeling foolish. Kris had been using his job to pick up women for as long as it had been up and running yet I was willing to air all of our dirty laundry to get him out of jail. I swallowed hard.

"Yes, Mr. Winchester. I'd like to put my divorce on hold and hire you to defend my husband."

He leaned back in his chair and looked at me for a moment before responding.

"Well, the Nannycam that you have that recorded your husband and your Nanny," he started.

"Delilah," I interjected.

"Wait, Delilah was your Nanny?" he asked, rubbing his chin.

"And she's my half-sister, but neither of them know that yet," I confessed.

"Oh boy," Mr. Winchester said.

"But, yes, I'm sure the Nannycam recorded the threesome we had just this afternoon."

"And you're sure you want me to defend him and not just use this to help accelerate the divorce?" he asked.

"I'm certain," I said, getting up, "I'll be back with the recording and the retainer."

# Tammy

Sam had lost her fuckin' mind puttin' her hands on Ty. If that bitch wasn't pregnant, I would tell Sheila to take me to her crib so I could whoop her ass. But her life was fucked up enough its own, she was still married to Anthony's trifling ass and now I knew that Tyrone was done with her ass.

I went into the bathroom and got some peroxide and cotton balls and a towel to put some ice in for his jaw. I walked back into the living room to find him sitting on the couch with his head in his hands. The sight tugged at my heart. I sat down next to him.

"Hey handsome," I said, putting my hand on his thigh.

"Hey beautiful," he said, looking at me with so much hurt in his eyes.

I poured some peroxide on a couple of cotton balls and dabbed his split lip. We didn't say anything while I treated his wounds. I watched his face and there was no response to the pain of his busted lip but his mind was in a million places. Then he looked at me and his face softened. I smiled at him and our eyes said what need not be said aloud. I touched his cheek and realized it was a bit swollen. I got up with the towel and went to fill it with ice.

When I came back to the couch, I blushed at the way Tyrone was watching me. I sat back down on the couch and he laid his head in my lap. I pressed the cold towel gently against his cheek.

"Talk to me, baby," I said, looking down at him.

Nel was in her room, probably trying on her thirtieth outfit for her date. I knew Tyrone wanted to talk but knew he wanted to avoid burdening me with his issues because I had shit of my own to sort through.

"I don't wanna dump my shit on you, love," he said, just like I knew he would.

"It's not dumpin' if I asked for it," I countered, "now, spill it."

He laughed softly, then let out a heavy sigh.

"It's just been a long week, baby."

"I know. First you get locked up for getting that looney ass bitch Delilah off Nel, then I get shot, and now this shit with Sam. You just can't catch a break with the women in your life, huh? It's a wonder you haven't lost your mind," I said.

"Yeah, and then that shit with Tanisha," he added.

"Tanisha?" I asked, knowing that I'd just heard that name from Nel. "Are you talking about your birth mother?"

"Yeah, our birth mother. She went to Nel's foster mom's house lookin' for her then showed up at her job. Then, after I convinced Nel to at least have lunch with her and she begged me to come along, I was treated like I was less than shit by the woman who abused and abandoned *me*."

"Oh wow," I said, at a loss for words. Nel had filled me in on some of the details, but hearing them from him hurt so much worse.

"I mean, can you imagine a woman who put me through what she's put me through treating me like I did something to her because of how I turned out?"

"Oh, I can," I said, thinking back to my own childhood.

My momma was embarrassed of me because I was mixed. One night, her and her bourgeois friends decided to slum it and went to a party at Tuskegee University. She had one too many and ended up sleeping with some random student. She didn't even remember his name.

When she came up pregnant, she kept me because she thought her fiancé could possibly have been my father. His father had oil money so she would have been set for life. They got married to avoid the embarrassment of people finding out that she was pregnant, but when I was born they took one look at me and knew that I wasn't his. They stayed together and had more children but I was sent off to my grandparents' house. I hated it there. They called me "the mud baby".

I was their little secret and was forced to hide in my room when they had dinner parties. I wasn't treated like family on the holidays. I was more like the help. My siblings went to the best schools and I was sent to whatever school the maid was zoned for. By the time I was old enough to speak up and possibly become a problem, I had been raised by the maid, Miss Taylor. She started bringing me home with her after work and, I found out later, my grandparents began to pay her to keep me there with her.

When I found out all of this, around the time that I was sixteen, I moved out. That's when I met Tre. I moved in with him and the rest was history. I leaned down and kissed Tyrone softly so that I didn't hurt his lip.

"I'm so sorry baby. I really am. At least she's back and that's a good thing, right?"

"I guess," he said, his brow furrowing, "after Nel went off on her at the restaurant about how she was treating me, she told us she had AIDS and wants to be with us as often as she can before she dies. Kinda make amends."

Nel had already told me all of this but hearing it from Ty, from his mouth, in his words, hit harder because I could hear the hurt in his tone.

"Damn," was the only thing I could think to say.

I started massaging his scalp trying to help him relax. It worked. He took a few heavy breaths and the next thing I knew he was asleep.

I turned on the TV and waited for Nel to make her exit, headed out on her date. Even if things didn't work out with this guy, I truly hoped that he showed her how a real man treated a woman. Like Tyrone had shown me. I leaned down, moving a stray loc from across his face, and kissed him on the forehead.

# Sheila

I was so nervous. I had tried on ten outfits and twice as many pairs of shoes. I finally settled on a yellow off-the-shoulders top, a pair of ripped jeans, and my yellow flat sandals. I was glad my pedicure still looked decent. I checked the time and realized that I was cutting it really close so I walked out of the bedroom to see if Tammy signed off on my choice.

I entered the living room to find Tyrone asleep in Tammy's lap, his feet hanging off the end of my couch. Tammy took her eyes off the television screen and took full inventory of my appearance.

"You look so pretty, Nel," she said, smiling.

"Yeah?" I asked, looking down at myself insecurely.

"I bet your room looks a mess," she laughed.

"You already know it does."

"Well, the mess was worth it. You're gonna have to teach me how to do that two color eye shadow thing," she said.

"Girl, in all of the years I've known you, I ain't never seen you wear makeup," I smiled at her compliment.

"Well, I might wanna start. Tre never let me wear makeup. I think he was worried that I'd attract somebody who would treat me right. I haven't gotten my hair done in ages."

"I think a girl's spa day is in order this weekend," I offered. "My treat."

"You're on," Tammy said, smiling. "I bet Ty is gonna flip his wig when he sees me all dolled up."

"You're beautiful just the way you are," Tyrone cracked his eyes and said.

"Awww, Bay," Tammy said, blushing.

"You two make me gag," I said, jokingly pretending to vomit.

"Don't be a hater all your life, Nel," Tyrone said, sitting up to kiss Tammy.

"She won't let us be great, will she, baby," Tammy said, looking at me with a sparkle in her eyes.

I laughed at them and headed out on my date. When I got in the car, I connected the Bluetooth and called Ron.

"Hey there," I said when he answered.

"Hey yourself. I thought you were gonna stand me up."

"No. I just had to choose the right outfit," I admitted, feeling silly for taking so long to get ready.

"I'm flattered that you put so much thought into it."

Well, first dates are a big deal. They can make or break the situation."

"True," he said, laughing. "Glad you finally admitted it's a date."

"Well it *is* isn't it? I mean, I've been out of the game for many years and it is a *weekday*, but we've already set a second date... so, yeah, this is a date in my opinion."

"And your opinion is of high importance to me," he said.

I blushed. He was really laying it on thick but I was loving every second of it.

"If you're trying to seal the deal for some ass tonight, you might want to say those lines for later date because that's a no-go," I said, laughing.

"So a brotha gotta be after some ass to give you a compliment," he asked, challenging me.

I got quiet. He burst out laughing but I knew he was dead serious.

"At least we're on the same page, then," I said, trying to save the conversation.

"I just texted you the address to our date night location," he said, "I'll see you in about twenty minutes."

"Ok."

At the red light, I checked my texts and saw the address was 299 Jay Street in Prattville. I wasn't familiar with the location so I plugged it into my GPS and let it guide me there. A chill came over me and I felt the need to call Anthony. He'd texted me earlier and I had been short with him, telling him that I was getting ready for my date, which I wasn't but it was my way of getting him to leave me alone. But now, I felt like something was wrong. I instructed my phone to dial his number. It rang once and went straight to voicemail. The box was full, which was probably a good thing because I didn't need to leave him a message. Immediately I felt stupid.

I drove, without music, to my destination. I was surprised to find that it was a park. The sign read "Overlook Memorial Park". I got out of my car and saw Ron standing at the gazebo, a trail of rose petals leading the way there. I saw candles lit and dinner in Tupperware containers. He had some smooth jazz instrumentals playing softly when I approached. I was impressed. He'd put a lot of thought into this date.

"Hey there, beautiful. I see you found it no problem."

I couldn't hide my smile. I was really blown away by the whole thing. I'd expected to be going to dinner at a restaurant or some other public place. But this set-up, even though it was in a park, was very private and intimate.

"I figured the best way to get to know you would be to spend time alone with you," he explained, motioning for me to take a seat. "At a restaurant, we'd have servers interrupting us and have to lean in just to hear one another over the hundreds of other voices in the room."

I took a seat, smiling harder as he poured my wine and put salad onto my plate.

"Did you make all this?" I asked, looking at the Tupperware containers sitting on the table.

"Yes. Just finished cooking when you called and told me you were on your way. I even brought a microwave just in case you got lost or something," he said, pointing to the microwave attached to the extension cord.

I laughed. I hadn't noticed the microwave. I could just see the crazy looks he must have gotten from his neighbors when he left his house carrying a microwave.

"We could have eaten at your house, you know. Saved you the manual labor of having to carry appliances around," I laughed again.

"We could have. But you just met me so I wasn't sure how comfortable you would have been with that. And your comfort level is a top priority for me. Besides," he said, pointing to the garden, "you can't enjoy natural beauty like this within the confines of one's home."

I nodded in agreement and was in complete awe of this man. He'd put so much effort into our date. I don't think a man had done anything like this for me in... well... ever. So I was going to enjoy every moment of it because it would only be a matter of time until he flipped the script on me. They always did.

I took a bite of my salad. It was lightly dressed. I smiled, realizing he'd really put in work. I toyed with the notion of sleeping with him but changed my mind. I wanted to see what his real end game was. He was gonna have to work for and wait on me. I still wasn't over Anthony as much as I wanted to be.

"You dressed this yourself?" I asked the obvious question, making small talk.

"Sure did," he said, beaming proudly.

"Impressive," I complimented, smiling.

"You always go out like this on a first date?"

"Only for the special ones," he said, looking me in the eyes.

We shared a gaze that gave me butterflies and made me wet all at the same time. *This man is something else*, I thought.

He got up and prepared our plates. I watched him scoop the shrimp and pasta with colorful vegetables onto the plates followed by garlic bread. They he plopped creamed potatoes on the side. I finished up my salad, ready for dinner. I took a forkful of the pasta and had to pause. The brotha could cook. I was highly impressed.

"So this is how you seal a business deal, huh?" I teased, tasting the potatoes and having to pause again.

"The business deal is already sealed," he said, swallowing his mouth full of food. "But when I meet such an impressive young woman I want to get to know better."

I blushed, feeling flattered. He was really laying it on thick but I was eating it the fuck up. Hell, if he wasn't for real, I was gonna ride this pampering train until it ran out of track.

We finished dinner and went for a walk in the garden. He asked me questions about myself and my life and I did the same. It felt amazing to be with a man who wasn't checking his phone and full of excuses. He was with me for as long as I wanted him to be. I could get used to this kind of treatment. But something was weighing heavy on my mind.

We had been sitting and talking, my feet ran his lap because they were starting to hurt. I looked at him and decided to lay it all out there.

"So do you date the women you work with often?" I posed the question.

"Usually, yes," he answered honestly and without hesitation.

"How does that usually work out for you?" I asked, probing deeper.

"It turns out well until jealousy becomes an issue. It's crazy. I've dated actresses, models, promoters, club owners, I believe in being with women who are in my field because they understand the hours I keep and the kind of work I have to do, you know?"

"Yeah, I know," I said, thinking back on Shawn and Tammy's words.

"But they are even more insecure than women who aren't in the field. I've seen all of these beautiful women morph into clingy, validation-seeking creatures. It was crazy."

"That sounds crazy. But I get it. Men aren't really comfortable with my job requirements, either. It's hard finding someone who understands," I confessed.

"I can see that. You're in the presence of powerful man with the money to buy and sell the average man several times. That can be an ego crusher. It takes a special kind of man, or woman for that matter, to handle what we do."

I just nodded my agreement.

"So, how did the relationships end and did it fuck up your business relationships once the love affair was over?"

"I'm a grown up, so I was always cool. But them, well they usually didn't take it very well."

"But you just asked me to dinner so are you a glutton for punishment or are you just insane?"

"I think I'm a little bit of both," he said, winking.

I giggled. He was a trip.

"I figured I'd keep trying my hand until I met one who got it. I knew she was out there but I never would've guessed that she'd be in Montgomery, Alabama."

I blushed for the hundredth time. He'd had me giggling and shit all night.

"So you think I'm that *one*?" I asked skeptically

"It's too early to tell. But I just feel like you're *different*. The rest I have to find out. I will say that I'm intrigued," he said.

He never broke eye contact. It made my stomach do a flip. He seemed to leap on the opportunity. He leaned forward and came within centimeters of my lips.

"Your lips look so soft I've been wanting to feel them all night. May I?" He asked permission to kiss me.

"Mmm hmmm," was all that I could get out.

He didn't wait for me to change my mind. He pressed his lips to mine and I closed my eyes and breathed in his breath. I opened my mouth, inviting his tongue in. He accepted the invitation and we kissed passionately. His hands never went below my shoulders. He held my face and I tangled my hands in his locs. My body temperature rose and I broke free, gasping for air.

"I think I should be getting home," I said, summoning every bit of self-control I had not to jump his bones.

"Are you sure? We can stop and just chill," he offered, sounding like he wasn't ready for me to go.

"I've got an early morning tomorrow. And we're still goin' out Friday night, right?" I asked, confirming our next date.

"Unless you allow me to take you to lunch before then."

"That would be nice. Do you need any help packing up your car?"

"No, I got it," he said standing up, a sad look on his face.

I almost felt guilty leaving him but I really had a long day tomorrow and needed to get back to Tammy.

"Look," I said, "I really like you and want to see you again. This isn't gonna be our last time seeing or talking to each other, and not just for business. Tonight was too perfect not to want to see what else you've got up your sleeve," I said, smiling genuinely.

We'd made it to my car and he opened the door for me.

"Please call me and let me know you made it home," he said, leaning in for another kiss. "If I don't answer, I'm probably lugging my microwave into the house," he joked.

I laughed and then closed the distance between our mouths. When we came up for air, I left my hand cupping his face.

"Thank you so much for tonight. Everything was so perfect," I said, gazing into his eyes.

"My pleasure," he replied. "I'll be seeing you soon."

"Indeed," I said, smiling and lowering into the driver's seat of my car.

"Wait," he said, remembering something. He jogged to the gazebo and came back with a single, long-stemmed rose and a manila envelope that I assumed held his signed promotion deal.

I smiled and waved goodbye before pulling out of my parking space. I didn't see anything on the way home. I was on cloud nine. I couldn't wait to tell Tammy all about it.

# Anthony

I sat in my cell, frustrated as hell. I couldn't be mad at anyone but myself because my dick got me into this shit. I wasn't even mad at Sam for the threesome. If I hadn't fucked Beth the night before, Sam wouldn't have made me call her. But I really felt like Beth was gonna accuse me of rape whenever I dumped her. The bitch was unstable. I hoped that Andrea called Sam and told her what was going on before she got to the house and saw the signed divorce papers. She may not come get me out if she found those first.

I looked through the bars at the gray concrete slabbed walls and had nothing but time to think. I thought about how I'd treated Samantha and all the other women in my life. How I let my dick make the majority of my decisions for me. How I'd really bit off more than I could chew this time because Beth had told me that Delilah's attorney was her father and I knew, if he thought I'd raped his daughter, he would be coming for blood. I know I would if it was one of my girls. It was already bad enough that she was fuckin' a black man. I'm sure he'd be more willing to accept that I'd forced myself on her than that she'd fucked me of her own free will.

I had to laugh. Hell, he'd had no problem defending Delilah so he was even willing to accept her fuckin' a black woman over fuckin' me. Of all the things that I could be locked up for, man, this here was some bullshit. Never in my life had I had to take pussy from a woman. They gave it to me eagerly. And not because I was the most handsome guy, either. But this mouthpiece that I had could persuade a nun to give up her goods. I told 'em what they wanted to hear. Made them feel like they were the only ones I wanted, the one I'd been waiting for my whole life.

Once you made a woman feel needed she was putty in your hands. I smiled at all the women I'd landed who were out of my league. All the ones who deserved better, more loyal men but fought for time with me. Like Sheila. Sheila was the kind of woman a man bought a ring for after the second date. She was the settle down, forever type of woman you built a world for. If she could get past her damage and see her worth, she never would have gotten involved with me. But she had and I'd taken her through all kinds of bullshit. I felt bad for hurting her but I couldn't do anything to her that she didn't allow me to. But still, she hadn't deserved to be hurt, left pregnant, and beat up the way she had been. But, then again, maybe that ass whoopin' was what she deserved after killing my baby. Yeah, I was fuckin' Delilah way before then, but for her to make that decision without even consulting me was fucked up.

I'd had no real plans on leaving Sam for Sheila. I was too damn comfortable for that. But she was a good Plan B. She could spoil me. And she did. She even stayed around after she found out about Sam and Delilah. I shook my head, making myself snap out of it. There was no use crying over spilled milk. I laid back on my mat on the floor. The jail was overcrowded so everyone didn't have a bed. And I didn't want one. I wasn't trying to get comfortable in this cage. I was gonna be outta here soon. I knew that either my sister or my wife would be here to get me anytime now.

"Bailey! Kristopher Bailey!" the officer called my name, making me jump up like I'd been struck by lightning.

"Right here," I said, getting up and walking to the front of the cell.

"Your attorney is here to see you," he said, opening the bars.

I held back a smile, trying not to show my excitement to be getting out of this cell just in case things didn't go the way I wanted them to and I ended up back in here. I followed the officer down the corridor and into the meeting area. An older white man with a shiny bald head stood up and extended his hand.

"Mr. Bailey, I'm Mark Winchester. Your wife Samantha hired me to defend you," he said as I shook his hand.

"Nice to meet you," I said, politely. "Am I gettin' outta here anytime soon," I cut to the chase.

"Let's get some details straight, first. But know that we are working to get you out of here," he said, pulling a legal pad and pen out of his briefcase. He flipped to a blank page.

"OK. What do you need to know? I didn't rape Beth. I'm an adulterer. I'm triflin'. I don't deserve my wife. But I am *not* rapist. Beth is upset because I told her that I didn't want to be with her," I explained.

"Being upset about being dumped is a far stretch from accusing someone of rape," Mr. Winchester said skeptically.

"Look, I know you're my wife's attorney. You drafted the divorce papers so I'm sure you're not my biggest fan. I'm an infidel, a doggish dude, but not a rapist. I don't have to rape nobody. The bitch is lyin'," I said, my blood beginning to boil.

"Ok," he said, making notes in his pad, "you may want to refrain from referring to her as a bitch if this goes to trial."

"*If* this goes to trial?" I asked, his choice of words catching my attention.

"Yes, I have been in touch with Miss Henry's attorney. Your wife brought video of your... ummm... threesome that was recorded on the Nannycam, that took place after the supposed assault."

"Nannycam?" I asked. I was learning new shit as he spoke.

"Yes, Mr. Bailey. Your wife installed it after she hired her half-sister a Miss..." he flipped through his legal pad to find the name, "Delilah Powell as your children's caretaker."

"*Half-sister?*" I asked. I knew I sounded like a complete fool repeating everything he said but my head was starting to pound. Samantha was maniacal. I found myself turned on and extremely angry at the same time.

Mr. Winchester grinned at me. His smugness angered me further but I kept my composure.

"Mr. Bailey, Samantha says that you may have texts from Miss Henry that would support our case," he said, getting back to the matter at hand.

"My phone," I said, thinking of where my phone was, "oh, it's at the house. I left it in the bedroom on the dresser. The cops took me outta the house and I didn't get the chance to grab it. When is she claiming I raped her?"

"She says the assault happened at Miss Powell's house when she was packing up her things. She said you followed her there after you accompanied her locksmith to help unlock her car. She said you made several advances towards her then showed up, uninvited, to the house, claiming to want to help."

"How did I know she was there if she didn't tell me? And why would she not accuse me of rape immediately after we had sex?" I asked getting angry again.

"These are the questions I've already posed. Once I have your phone, I believe we can get the charges dropped and the case dismissed. We'll see what happens at your bail hearing tomorrow," he said, packing his things.

"Tomorrow?" I asked. "So I'm staying in here tonight?"

"Unfortunately, yes," he said, getting up, "but you should be a free man tomorrow."

"Ok," I said, waiting for the guard to come and escort me back to my cell.

I had a lot of thoughts racing through my head. Sam was dangerous. I needed to decide whether or not I could be faithful to her because the game she was playing could have me locked up for the rest of my life... or dead somewhere. I sat in jail unable to sleep, thinking about Beth and Delilah and how Sam had found a way to connect herself to and eliminate both. Then I thought about Sheila and realized that Sam was fuckin' her brother and now havin' his twins. It was too much to consider a coincidence. This was some real six degrees of separation shit. Yeah, Sam's ass was dangerous.

I watched the sky begin to change colors. I knew they would be coming to get me soon. I just hoped that the lawyer was able to get my phone and I could get out of this cage once and for all. Then my wife and I were gonna have a talk.

# Tyrone

I was laid across the couch, my head in Tammy's lap. She was watching TV and massaging my scalp but my mind was elsewhere. I was angry with Sam and even angrier that I was stuck with her crazy ass for the next eighteen years. I was worried about Tammy. I knew she was in love with me, but she was loyal so I wanted to give her the chance to decide whether or not she was truly done with Tre. I couldn't help but wonder what Scooter had been doing at their house.

What was really weighing on me was how my mom had treated me. Even though she'd changed her tune once Nel had handed her ass to her in front of everyone at the restaurant, the way she'd acted in the beginning had hurt. It was like I was a disgrace or something and like nothing that I'd turned out to be was her fault. My heart ached a little bit. I didn't realize I was crying until Tammy said something.

"Baby, what's wrong?" she asked.

"What? Nothing," I lied.

"Tyrone Price! You aren't gonna sit in my face and lie to me. You're crying. What the hell is going on in that head of yours?"

I reached up and wiped the tears from my eyes. I sat up and looked at her, deciding how honest to be with her. I chose to lay it all out there.

"It's a lot," I said, nervous about opening up to her.

"Let me see how good my Ty reading skills are," she said, jokingly. "You're worried about me and... you're wishing you weren't stuck with Sam's ass and... hmmm," she paused, thinking, "You're thinking about the situation with Tanisha, right?"

"Woman, you are amazing!" I said, unable to hide my smile.

"I just know my man," she said, leaning over to kiss me.

"Your man, huh?" I asked, raising an eyebrow. "So what about Tre? I know you, too. You don't just walk away like that."

"Baby, I'm so over Tre's ass. I gave him *years* and what did I get out of it? Cheated on, an STD that left me infertile, regular ass whoopins. The best thing that came out of me knowing Tre was meeting you, Nel, and having Jeffrey in my life. If you hadn't been there that day, he probably would have killed me."

"Let's be real Tam, he started beatin' on you *because* of me, so technically I saved you from a situation I put you in," I pointed out.

"Come on Ty, don't do that. If it wasn't you, it would have been something else that set him off. He had it in him."

"I guess. So, how do you feel about Scooter comin' over there?" I asked, wanting to get her take on the situation.

"I'm scared shitless," Tammy admitted, her hazel eyes getting wide. "I really do feel like he was there to finish the job. I remember him and Tre promising to never leave witnesses. They have to dismiss the case if there are no witnesses."

"Oh wow," I said in shock, "so you think they were serious? Like he'd really try to kill you?"

"Yep, especially now that he knows I took the money."

"Money? What money, baby?" I asked, completely lost.

"The cash stash. It was their bail and skip town money in case one of them got caught up. Scooter was going to get the money and bail Tre out, then they were comin' for me and gonna skip town as soon as they killed me," she said, sounding frightened.

"Well, I won't let that happen," I promised, patting her thigh and looking into her eyes lovingly, planning to get her a lawyer in the morning.

"I know you won't. But this isn't about me. Tell me how you're feeling about the whole Sam situation."

"I don't know, baby. She put her fuckin' hands on me today like she'd lost her mind. If she wasn't a woman and pregnant with my children, man," I shook my head.

"But that's why she did it, Hun. She knew you weren't gonna hit her back. That bitch pulled that shit after I was gone because I woulda tapped that ass with my good arm," she said, her face turning red.

I laughed at the sight. She was so cute when she got angry. Her face turned red and her lips got tight. Her eyes went from green to a dark brown.

"It wouldn't have come to that," I said, still smiling. "But I'm still having children with this woman, this married woman that I was just havin' fun with. I don't know how she's gonna act now that she's on the warpath and back with Anthony. I'm gonna get a lawyer in the morning for me and for you. We both need to know what our options are."

"Ok," she said with a frustrated sigh.

"I know, baby. I don't want to go through all this shit, either. But we're dealin' with some fools. I can't go back to prison. I'm gonna make the system work for me... for *us* this time," I said matter-of-factly.

"I gotcha. It's just... I don't know, this is all too much."

Now *she* was crying. I could understand. Her whole world had been flipped upside down and now she was worried that her life was in danger. I reached over and pulled her close. I let her get it all out. I knew she was hurting. I was hurting *for* her. I held her as tightly as I could, making sure that I didn't hurt her arm. When she finally stopped shaking, I got up to get her a bottle of water. She drank the whole thing without stopping.

"How's your arm feeling?" I asked, concerned.

It's okay. My medicine is still working well," she said sniffling, trying to compose herself.

She shifted, rotating her arm just a little to show me that she was regaining her mobility. I smiled, proud of how strong she really was. This woman had walked the path to hell barefoot and hadn't let it kill her positivity. She was amazing and, in just a matter of time, she was going to be all mine. Then a feeling came over me that I'd never felt before.

"Marry me," I said, looking Tammy in the face.

She looked like she stopped breathing. She turned her head to the side and looked at me like I was insane.

"What?" she asked to make sure she'd heard me right.

"Tamara Alexander, I have loved you from the moment I laid eyes on you. I waited for more than a decade for you to rid yourself of that poison you called a relationship. I don't want to wait another moment. Will you please marry me?" I asked, getting off of the couch and onto one knee.

"Tyrone, quit playin'! Are you bein' for *real* right now?" she asked in disbelief.

"I'm serious as a damn heart attack. We can go to the courthouse tomorrow, me, you, Nel, and Jeff, the only ones that matter. If you say yes, I'll get your ring tonight and make it official. So, what do you say?"

"Boy, you know the answer! Yes! Hell yes I'll marry you," she said, jumping up from her seat.

"Good," I said, standing up and kissing her. "Let me go get your ring."

"What the hell is goin' on here?" Nel asked from the doorway to the kitchen. I didn't know she was there.

"Ty just asked me to marry him and I said yes!" Tammy screamed, running over to her.

"Oh, I heard," my sister said shooting me a look.

I just smirked back at her.

"I'm going to get the ring and we're goin' to the courthouse tomorrow. Can you and Jeff come?" I asked.

"I'm sure he'd love to be there. He may be a little confused though, seeing that he didn't know about you and Tammy. Matter of fact, I'll come with you to pick out the ring," she said smirking.

"That would be awesome!" Tammy yelled not catching the looks that were being passed back and forth. "Make sure he gets a big one," she said, winking at Nel.

"Oh, I will," she said, the undertone in her speech making me flinch like a child in trouble.

Tammy walked back towards the couch, stopping to give me a long kiss before going back to the couch sitting down. The look of elation on her face was priceless. I felt better than I had in a very long time. I looked down at my sister and got butterflies in my stomach. I knew I was in for a long talk.

"Well, go put on your shoes. We've got about an hour before the jewelry store closes," she said, looking at her watch.

"Yes ma'am," I said jokingly, walking over to the couch to slide on my shoes.

"And Tammy, when we get back, we'll plan a girl's day tomorrow instead of this weekend so you're ready for your *big day*. I'll cancel all of my appointments and Ty," she said looking at me firmly, "you get the pleasure of checking Jeff out and explaining how you and Tammy found yourselves engaged."

I laughed nervously. I would be up all night trying to figure out how to explain the situation to my nephew. I was more nervous about that than the fact that I was going to be a married man this time tomorrow.

Nel and I walked out the door.

"We taking my car or yours?" I asked.

"Yours," she said shortly.

I pressed my keyless entry and we both got in. Before I could crank up the car, she turned and punched me in the shoulder as hard as she could.

"Have you lost your damn mind? As much as that woman has been through, you gonna drag her into your bullshit? You couldn't wait a couple of months? Hell, a couple of *years*?" she yelled.

She was yelling so loud my ears were ringing. I sat there, rubbing my shoulder. She'd hit me hard as hell.

"Damn, what is it with women hitting me today?" I yelled frustrated. "Look Nel, I know this is abrupt but I've been waiting forever for Tammy to be free of Tre's ass. I've wanted her for a long time. She's a good woman and deserves a good man. I can be good to Tammy. I'm ready to be with one woman. To settle down. The only reason I got involved with Sam's ass at all was because Tammy was with Tre. She's done with him now and after tonight I'm done with Sam's crazy ass. All I want is to see my kids and be in their lives. I'm going to do that, even if I gotta get a lawyer to make it happen."

"You're for real, huh?" my sister asked, her face softening.

"I'm dead ass serious. I love her, Nel. I've never met a woman like her. I don't even care about her not being able to have children. I just want *her*."

"Well, let's go get a ring! What's your budget?"

"For Tammy, there is no budget," I said, meaning every word.

"All right now, deep pockets," she teased, "your sugar mama done cut you off, you better start revamping your budget."

I cranked up the car and pulled off. She was telling the truth. I needed to make some changes, starting with this car and then moving out of that apartment. I didn't know how much money Tammy had gotten from her house but I knew how much I had saved. I figured that, plus our incomes would be enough to buy a house. My wife deserved a house. And it would definitely be a good look when I took Samantha to court about my children.

I headed down Vaughn Road towards Jared's. I was ready to make Tammy mine, 'til death do us part. I even considered inviting Tanisha. She's family and since she was dying, I might as well make her part of his much as I could.

"I think I want to invite Tanisha," I shared my thought aloud with my sister.

"That's sweet!" she said smiling, "especially after the way she treated you today. I wouldn't be mad if you never want to see her again."

"She's our mother, Nel. And she's dying. She really hurt my feelings today, especially after all the shit she did to me as a child, but you can go to hell holding a grudge. I'd rather show her the love and kindness she never showed me. Everyone deserves a little kindness," I said, parking.

"You're better one than me. After the way she did you today, I wouldn't piss on her ass if she was on fire if I was you," she said, rolling her neck.

"Oh, I know. So did everyone else in the damn restaurant this afternoon," I laughed as we walked up to the store.

"Shut up, Ty," she said as I opened the door for her.

We walked in, laughing, as I prepared to commit myself and my life to my one true love.

*****

The next morning, after I got my hair retwisted and braided, I went to get Jeff from school. We were both gonna get new suits and lunch before heading to the courthouse. I figured I could explain things to him and answer any questions he had. I hope he'd be happy for us. He was a good kid so I figured he would.

When he walked into the office, his brow bent with concern. I stood up and flashed him a huge smile. He relaxed a little.

"Everybody's aight, nephew," I reassured him, "I've got a surprise for you."

"Okay," he said, following me out of the office and out of the school.

"I'm getting married," I said, unlocking the car.

"Really? That's what's up, Uncle Ty!" he said excitedly. "Who is she? Do I know her?"

"Well, that's the thing," I said, checking my rearview mirror before backing out of my parking spot. "It's Tammy."

"I *knew* it!" Jeff yelled laughing.

"You knew what?" I asked, shocked at his reaction.

"I knew y'all were more than friends," he said smiling and reclining his seat.

"And how did you know that?" I asked, laughing at the fact that I was the one asking all the questions.

"Come on Unc, I pay attention," he said sounding offended.

"I gotcha, youngin'," I laughed. "You just made this whole situation easier on me. Let's go get some suits and something to eat. Then to the courthouse and to meet your grandmother."

"Grandmother?" he repeated, sounding confused.

"Yeah, she found us after all these years and she's sick so your mom and I wanna make the most of the time she has left."

"Yes sir," he said thoughtfully.

"Tell me what's on your mind, nephew."

"I just don't know if I wanna meet that lady. She wasn't a mother to you and momma. I'm sorry she's sick but our lives shouldn't have to change because of it," he said folding his arms across his chest.

"You are your mother's child," I said laughing at how much he sounded like Nel right then.

"I'm just bein' real, Unc," he said forcefully.

"Well, let's talk about it, ok," I offered, "maybe I can change your mind."

"I doubt it, but ok," he said.

I knew I had my work cut out for me. This boy was cut from the same stubborn ass cloth his mother was. But I hoped I could at least get him to give Tanisha a chance. Even though she didn't deserve one.

# Samantha

I sat, nervously, in the waiting area of the Montgomery Police Department, patting my foot and chewing on my nails. I'd met Mr. Winchester there because he was meeting with my husband. Then we were gonna make sure he had everything he needed for the bail hearing tomorrow. I'd hoped that we could get this shit resolved tonight and I could bring my husband home. The children were really upset. I needed their dad home so that they would know that everything was okay.

It was getting late so I texted Andrea and asked if the kids could stay with her. She replied that they were already in the bed. I smiled. She was a lifesaver. I felt bad about all of this and how it was impacting my children. As if my work schedule wasn't bad enough, I'd just up and left to shack up with Tyrone, Kris's ass was always in the streets chasing hoes, and now I was about to have another man's babies. Then, they had to see their dad escorted out of the house in handcuffs. They had to be traumatized. My eyes filled with tears the more I thought about it. They deserved better, from both of us. And I was definitely gonna get them, and us, some counseling.

I was about to get up and start pacing when Mr. Winchester walked out into the lobby.

"So..." I asked, anxiously.

"Mr. Bailey says his phone is one the dresser at your house. And I had to let him know about Miss Powell being your sister and about the Nannycam. I needed him completely in the loop in case there were some questions asked by the prosecuting attorney. I'm sure he's going to have questions for you if they release him," he informed me, massaging his temples.

"*If* they release him? I'm paying you a lot of money, I need more than an if," I said looking him square in the face.

"There are a lot of factors coming into play here. I can't guarantee anything here but that I will present a strong defense for your husband. Can you get the phone for me and meet me at my office?" he asked, walking towards the door.

"I've got it right here," I said reaching into my purse. "I grabbed it on my way up here in case he said there was something in there we could use."

He stopped walking and turned around. I handed the phone to him and saw the look on his face that said he hoped he'd never see us again once this was all over. I knew I would have to find someone else to handle my divorce but since I wasn't planning on getting divorced anymore, I didn't care. I just wanted my husband home.

"I'll see you at my office at seven thirty tomorrow morning. We'll head over here in time for his bail hearing at nine," he said before turning to leave without waiting for my response.

I walked out behind him and got in my car. I wanted to kick Beth's ass but knew that wouldn't do me any good. I just accepted that karma was kicking my husband's ass and hoped this would be enough to make him keep his dick in his pants. All those other women he'd been with, even his baby mamas and the only person here trying to get him out of jail was me. I felt stupid, kinda like my momma waiting on my daddy to get right. She died waiting. I wasn't gonna die waiting on Kris. If he didn't get right after this, I would be done. For good.

I pulled into my driveway, wondering how many of my neighbors had seen my husband dragged out of my house and put into a police cruiser. I had dealt with so much embarrassment with Kris you'd think I'd be used to it by now. But that kind of embarrassment you can never get used to.

I walked into my empty house and sat at the table. There was a folder on the table I hadn't noticed the last time I was home because I was in such a rush to get back to the lawyer's office. I opened it and found the divorce papers my husband must have had drawn up before he got arrested. But unlike mine, his were signed. My heart started to thud in my chest. Tears streamed down my cheeks. Everything he'd put me through and I hadn't been as eager to get rid of him as he had been to get rid of me.

I picked up my phone and started to call Tyrone. Then I realized I couldn't call him because of our blow-up today. I was pretty sure he was done with me. I decided to text him instead.

**Me:** *I'm sorry. I miss you.*

**Tyrone:** *I'm getting married tomorrow.*

My eyes grew as big as my head. I knew I couldn't be seeing things clearly.

*Who the fuck was he marrying?* I asked myself the obvious question. I knew it was that bitch Tammy. Here I was, pregnant with his children, on the brink of losing my marriage trying to build something with him, and he jumps at the chance to marry that barren, ratchet ass trap bitch as soon as she became single. All of the time and money I'd invested was down the drain. And now that bitch was gonna be sleeping in the bed I bought, in the apartment I'd been paying for, and ridin' around in the car that I'd gotten him. I was fuckin' livid.

My first mind was to go to his house and show the fuck out but I changed my mind. I went online and stopped my autopay on his rent and his car note. In the morning, I would schedule an abortion. I didn't want the three I had. I sure as hell wasn't gonna have two more and be forced to see Tyrone and Tammy living in wedded bliss while I was with my no good ass husband. After I cancelled everything I was paying for Tyrone, I went back to our text thread and sent a final message before turning off my phone.

**Me**: *Congratulations. I'm having an abortion.*

I slammed my phone onto the table and went into the bedroom to set the alarm clock on the night stand to wake me up in the morning. I turned the volume up on the clock radio so that I could hear it and snuggled beneath my covers to sleep alone, something that had become the norm in my life. I began to cry. Nothing I did was good enough. No one wanted me. Before I dozed off, I heard my doorbell ring. I started to ignore it but something was pulling at me to see who it was.

Hoping it was Tyrone coming to beg me not to murder our children, I threw on my robe and dragged myself to the door. My face got hot when I saw Beth's ass standing on the other side of my glass door.

"What the fuck do *you* want?" I asked, fighting the urge to snatch her into my living room and molly whop her ass.

"I want you," she said, very seriously.

"You want *what*?" I asked, unable to hide my confusion.

"Can I come in so we can talk?" she asked.

My better judgement told me to say no and slam the door in her face but I was lonely and in need of attention. And I was curious to hear what she had to say. I knew I didn't want Beth but I wanted someone there with me. Someone to make me feel desirable. I opened the door and stepped to the side to let her in.

"Before we talk about anything else, you need to drop the charges against Kris," I said emphatically.

"Done. I'll call my lawyer first thing in the morning. Right here so you can hear me. I just needed him out of the way so that I could get who I really wanted," she said, switching her ass into my house and towards my bedroom.

At that moment, I thought about Kris and Tyrone and every other man who had done me wrong my whole life, going back to my dad.

*Fuck 'em. Fuck 'em all,* I thought to myself before going into my bedroom and fucking Beth until we both collapsed, shaking onto the bed. I fell asleep, my head nestled between her breasts. This just felt right but in my mind I knew my children had been through enough. They didn't need a lesbian mother to add to their trauma. Not yet anyway.

I would get Beth to drop the charges, fuck her on the side until I knew my children were okay, and then if I liked her as a person, I would introduce them to her. We'd let the rest work itself out. If things worked out that way. As I dozed off, I made up my mind to do what made *me* happy despite how it made anyone else feel. That's how they all did me, even this bitch I was laid up with now.

# Tammy

I sat with my left hand extended, looking at my engagement ring as I got my pedicure. I couldn't believe that in a few short hours, I was going to be Mrs. Tyrone Price. Nel looked at me and started laughing.

"I take it you like the ring, huh?"

"Three carat, princess-cut solitaire, you damn right I like it," I said smiling from ear-to-ear.

"This is all so unreal to me," she said shaking her head.

"I know right," I responded. "I never would have thought that Ty and I would not just get the chance to be together, but make the commitment to love one another for the rest of our lives."

"Yeah but, you don't think this is all too fast?" she finally asked the question I knew was eating her up.

"Nel, Tyrone and I have been knowing one another for a very long time. This is not something that's happening overnight. Yes, Ty and I were just with other people. Yes, we do have our baggage. But, who doesn't?"

"If you're sure, then I'm behind you two one hundred and fifty percent," she said skeptically, "I just don't want either of you to get hurt."

"Thank you, hun, that's sweet. Neither one of us wants to see the other one hurt, either. But we're in love with each other. This is what getting married is. Two people who are deeply in love and want to be together unconditionally until the end of their lives," I explained, growing tired of having to explain myself.

"All right then, next were going dress shopping. My mother, Tanisha, is gonna meet us at David's Bridal. You might as well get to see the fool from which we came," she laughed and I got butterflies.

I realized that this was really real. I couldn't help but hope that Ty was having good luck with Jeff and he wasn't too confused by this whole thing. He was a smart kid so I wouldn't be surprised if he'd known about our feelings for each other all along. I'd spoken with Tyrone and he sounded like he had a lot on his mind. I figured he was planning for the day but something told me it was more. Since Nel had chased him out of her house last night, making him go home so he didn't see me until we got to the courthouse, then taken my phone and made me get some sleep, we hadn't talked until today.

I decided to shoot him a text and a picture of myself.

**Me:** *Spa day is going well. I'm so ready to begin this journey through life with you.*

**Ty** *Baby:* *You look beautiful, as always. Jeff and I are suit shopping. Honeymoon trip planned and pay for. Can't wait to say I do to you.*

I smiled and looked at Nel who was chilling with her head tilted back and cucumbers over her eyes.

"Texting my brother?" she asked, a smile coming across her face.

"You know it," I smiled, leaning back into the massage chair, relaxing. "How is your date last night?"

"Nothing short of amazing! The brotha cooked Shrimp Primavera with creamed potatoes and garlic bread. He had a perfectly dressed salad and a chilled bottle of wine. There were rose petals leading the way to the pavilion at the park where he had everything set up. He even brought his microwave in case I got lost on the way there," she gushed.

"Ooh, sounds like he went all out. And didn't even try to get no ass, did he?" I pointed out.

"Nope. He even asked permission before he went in for a kiss. He massaged my feet after we walked to the flower garden talking and everything it was..." She stopped talking when her phone went off. "Speak of the devil and..."

"He'll jump out of the pit every time," I smiled as she answered the phone.

I leaned back into my massage chair and toned out her conversation. It was none of my business. Her giggles broke through, making me smile. I hoped this dude was genuine. She deserved to be happy. Hell after the lives we've had, we all did. I smiled knowing that my happiness began at three thirty this afternoon. It couldn't get here fast enough.

*****

We walked into David's Bridal and I knew Tanisha Price as soon as I saw her. They both had her eyes. Sheila looked more like her than Ty did but I could see the resemblance in both. She had a broad smile across her face, showing her open-faced gold tooth. The light reflected off her platinum-blonde hair. I was just happy she seemed happy to be there after Nel had briefed me on their meeting yesterday.

"Penelope!" She shouted across the store in a smoker's raspy voice.

"Hey Tanisha... Mama," Nel still struggled with what to call her.

"And you must be Tammy," she said turning her attention to me as we finally got close enough not to have to yell across the store.

"Yes ma'am, Miss Price. I'm Tammy, nice to meet you."

She wrapped me into a bear hug that felt like it lasted forever. I was glad I'd taken my pain pills because she'd paid my brace no attention.

"Mama, her arm," Nel yelled pointing out the obvious.

"Oh my goodness. I'm sorry. I'm just so happy. What happened to your arm, child?"

"My ex shot me," I admitted.

"But aren't you pregnant? Why would he do something like that?"

I laughed, realizing she had no idea what the hell was going on aside from Tyrone getting married.

"I'll explain everything to you while Tammy picks out some dresses to try on," Sheila interjected.

I was grateful that she did because I felt a headache coming on. I took my cue to walk away. I knew I wanted a simple dress. Nel had insisted on coming here. She was paying for everything, which I appreciated, but I still went straight for the clearance rack.

As soon as I got there, I saw a classic-looking gown with a sweetheart neckline that hung to my knees. It would hug my curves but I was worried about the bandage that was on my shoulder. I kept looking and found a toga-style gown with the long sleeve on my left side so that the bandage would be covered. It was a mini-dress but it was flowing and flirty. I grabbed it and ran to the dressing room. It was perfect. I walked out and the looks on both Nel and Tanisha's faces let me know that they agreed.

"Leave it to your ass to find the perfect dress on your first try," Nel smiled, shaking her head.

"This is just fate manifesting," I said feeling like everything was just falling into place.

Tanisha hurried away, coming back with an orchid bouquet and a pair of pearl teardrop earrings.

"Oh, those are perfect," Nel beamed.

"Yeah they are," I giggled.

"Now, to my house to do your hair and makeup, huh?"

"Yes, ma'am," I said, fighting back the tears. "After we meet Ty downtown to fill out the license forms."

"Can I come?" Tanisha asked. "I got my dress and heels in the car. I'd love to be there to help you get ready."

"Of course," I said without a second thought. "Follow us to Nel's house and then we'll head downtown."

Her smile was priceless. This day was going to be a day of love and family. Who knew, maybe my mom had checked her messages and would show up. I could hope, but I wasn't holding my breath. Either way, this was about to be the happiest day of my life. I was about to become Mrs. Tyrone Price and Nel's sister.

# Tyrone

Jeff and I met Tammy, Tanisha, and Nel downtown to fill out the marriage license application. They were hell-bent on getting it done before the ceremony so that I didn't see Tammy again until she walked down the aisle. I hadn't told Tammy about Sam's threat to get an abortion because I didn't want to ruin our day. Besides, as much as it sucks, it was her body so it was her choice. As fucked up as it sounded, I wasn't as sad about it as I probably should have been. I would be rid of her and all the drama I knew was coming my way because I was marrying Tammy.

I'd already changed the rent and car payments over to my account this morning. I'd sort out what to keep and what to downgrade later. I just knew I didn't want any negative marks on my credit when I started looking for a house for myself and my new wife. I figured if Sam hadn't changed everything over already, she would soon.

When Tammy walked in, followed by my sister and my mom, my heart skipped a beat. She was gonna be my wife in a matter of hours. I was more ready than I had ever been to do anything in my life. We filled out the paperwork and I paid the fee. I barely had enough time to get a quick kiss before she was whisked away to get ready. Jeff and I shared a look and a laugh at how long it takes women to do stuff like that. Then we went to get his hair cut and to grab something to eat.

He'd helped me choose our honeymoon trip. Ten days, three each in London, Paris, and Rome. I was gonna get Nel to work with her realtor to get this beautiful house I'd found in Old Cloverdale purchased and ready for move-in when we got back. I planned to meet with the apartment manager about breaking my lease in the morning and we'd leave for New York on Friday. I was grateful that I was able to do all of this on such short notice and ironically, I had Sam to thank for that.

I thought about texting her but decided against it. I hated the way things had gone between us because I really did care for her. But I knew this was gonna end at some point. She was married. She wasn't supposed to get pregnant. It had all become this terrible roller coaster. But now it was over. I was marrying the love of my life. And she was still married with no temptation from me to coax her away from her husband anymore.

Jeff and I went to University Barbara Shop and I had Boo Man hook him up. He'd been my barber for years so I knew he'd get my nephew right and he didn't disappoint. Then we went downtown and ate at Chris's Hot Dogs. They had some of the best burgers in the city challenged only by Hamburger King. When we'd placed our order, Jeff started speaking truth beyond his age.

"Unc, you know my daddy is gonna be mad when he finds out about you and Miss Tammy getting married, right?"

"I know lil' man, but very few things in this world scare me and your daddy ain't one of them."

Jeff nodded thoughtfully. He sipped on his Arnold Palmer like he was choosing his words before continuing.

"Am I wrong for never wanting to see him again? I mean I don't like who he is and I really don't like him hurting her like that."

"Naw, you're not wrong. You need to tell your mama exactly how you feel and she'll make sure she does everything in her power to keep them away from you," I said wanting to let him know that his voice mattered.

"Okay. I'm gonna tell her tonight. So, are you nervous? I know they say guys get nervous before they get married," he asked, changing the subject.

"I'm just the opposite, nephew. I'm excited to marry Tammy. I've loved her a long time. Longer than you've been alive," I admitted.

"Dang, that's a long time," he said, shaking his head. "So why didn't you try to take her from daddy?"

"Because she wanted to be there. I don't steal, especially not women. I wanted her to want to leave her situation and choose to be with me. That way there would never be any questions about her wanting to go back to Tre," I said.

Thoughts of Sam crossed my mind again. I felt guilt pulling at me when I realized I had just entertained the notion of taking her from Anthony, even thought about marrying her. Just then, my phone lit up. I checked my messages and Sam had just sent me a text.

**Samantha:** *Abortion done. We no longer have any ties. I'm sure you're happy to be rid of me. Congratulations to Mr. and Mrs. Price.*

I didn't even respond. I had no energy to entertain the foolishness. If she'd had an abortion, there was nothing I could say to change it. I knew she was hurting but she could rely on her husband to console her.

"You okay, Uncle Ty?" Jeff snapped me out of my thoughts.

The server brought our food just in time.

"Yeah," I lied, "eat up, lil' man. I'm getting married in an hour. We still got to get dressed."

We ate and rushed to my apartment to get dressed. We got to the courthouse at three fifteen and I gave the magistrate a copy of Eric Benet and Tamia's "Spend My Life With You" to play when Tammy marched down the aisle.

I stood beside Jeff, both of us in matching navy blue Polo suits with blue and white pinstriped ties and cream Stacy Adams. My mom stood at the door in a teal green gown that flowed to the floor and a sequined shawl. She had a white orchid into her shoulder. She had a wide smile plastered on her face. She opened the door and my sister walked into the doorway wearing a dress that matched my mother's. She was holding half a dozen white roses and did her bridesmaid two-step until she reached me. She kissed Jeff on the cheek, touched my shoulder, and then took her place on the other side of the magistrate.

The magistrate nodded to the woman operating the CD player. She pressed play. I turned around and felt my chest poke out when I saw Tammy standing there. She looked beautiful! She had chosen a dress that covered the bandage on his shoulder but showed her legs. She had on heels that showed all of the definition from her calves to her thighs. In all the years I'd known Tammy, I'd never seen her in heels. She was a jeans and tennis shoes kinda girl. But I could definitely get used to her in heels and skirts.

Her hair was pinned up off of her shoulders with a few curly strands falling into her face and down her back. She had makeup to match my mama's and sister's dresses on her eyes and her lips were shiny but had no extra color. I couldn't take my eyes off of her as she inched closer and closer to me. When she finally got to me, I took her hand and took one long look into her tear-filled eyes before turning to the magistrate.

"Please begin so that I can spend the rest of my life with this beautiful woman," I pleaded.

The magistrate laughed before beginning our wedding ceremony. I smiled, not taking my eyes off of Tammy for a second. I recited my vows proudly and wiped her tears away as she recited hers to me. When he told me I could kiss the bride, I did. But it wasn't like any kiss I'd shared with Tammy, or Sam, or anyone else before. I was kissing my wife, my soulmate. I was sealing my forever and it felt damn good.

# Epilogue

*Delilah*

*Three months later...*

"Inmate 4682537," the Correctional Officer called my number.

I jumped off my bunk, knowing my time had finally come. I'd been in this fuckin' cell for ninety days and two weeks. I'd gotten the extra time added on for whoopin' this hooker bitch's ass for trying to steal my food stash outta my pillow case.

I walked to the front of the cell and waited while she opened the bars and walked in. I had all of my bedding in my arms and showed her my bracelet so that she could confirm I was the person she'd been looking for.

We walked to the front of the jail, where they do the intake and she took my bedding, putting it into a big, cloth rolling basket to be washed. She handed me a bag filled with the clothes I'd had on when they arrested me for kicking Sheila's ass. I got dressed and smiled, knowing Beth was out there waiting for me. She'd visited me religiously while I was locked up. Kept me up-to-date with everything that had been going on. Told me how Tre had shot Tammy and how Scooter had gotten locked up for bein' in their house waitin' to kill Tammy after she'd gotten out of the hospital.

She told me his baby mama left his ass in there to rot. Took all his money and their kids and moved to Florida with this nigga she'd been fuckin' with off Facebook. I knew that bitch wasn't loyal. She told me how she'd gotten Anthony locked up for rape so she could get close to Sam and now had that bitch cakin' her. Sam and Anthony were still married and Sam had aborted Tyrone's twins and quit the Kia Plant to avoid the embarrassment of having to see Tammy and Tyrone in marital bliss.

The best tidbit she'd told me, though, was that Sheila had landed herself this hot promoter who had just moved to the Gump and they were planning the Grand Opening of the Mojo Lounge in a couple of weeks. They'd tried to buy me out of the venture but I wasn't hearing that shit. Anthony and Tyrone had buried the hatchet now that Tyrone wasn't fuckin' Sam anymore. And they were more concerned about makin' money than beefin' over pussy anyway.

I walked out of the jail and saw Beth's fire red hair blowing in the wind as she sat on the steps smoking a cigarette. I cleared my throat and she turned around, jumped up, flicked the cigarette, and leapt up the steps towards me. I opened my arms and welcomed her as she threw herself up against me, covering my face with kisses.

I grabbed her ass. I had only one thing in mind.

"Everything ready?" I asked.

"Yes, baby," she smiled, cooing at me. "Anthony will meet us at the house in an hour. That gives us plenty of time to..."

She gave me a deep tongue kiss and I squeezed her ass tighter before whispering in her ear.

"Come on baby, I've been dyin' to taste you," I said, sticking my tongue in her ear.

We walked to the car and I grinned. I was ready to get some pussy. Anthony, who was pissed at Sam for not telling her that we were sisters, was planning to get his revenge on her. And I was gonna get Sheila's ass, once and for all. Starting with her new man.

## To Be Continued...